Natalie ~

At Your Service

JEN MALONE

go big or go home!,

Jen Malone

ALADDIN M!X
New York London Toronto Sydney New Delhi

This book is a work of fiction. Any references to historical events, real people, or real places are used fictitiously. Other names, characters, places, and events are products of the author's imagination, and any resemblance to actual events or places or persons, living or dead, is entirely coincidental.

ALADDIN M!X
Simon & Schuster Children's Publishing Division
1230 Avenue of the Americas, New York, NY 10020
First Aladdin M!X edition August 2014
Text copyright © 2014 by Jennifer Malone
Cover illustration copyright © 2014 by Annabelle Metayer
All rights reserved, including the right of reproduction in whole or in part in any form.
ALADDIN is a trademark of Simon & Schuster, Inc., and related logo is a registered trademark of Simon & Schuster, Inc.
ALADDIN M!X and related logo are registered trademarks of Simon & Schuster, Inc.
For information about special discounts for bulk purchases, please contact Simon & Schuster Special Sales at 1-866-506-1949 or business@simonandschuster.com.
The Simon & Schuster Speakers Bureau can bring authors to your live event.
For more information or to book an event contact the Simon & Schuster Speakers Bureau at 1-866-248-3049 or visit our website at www.simonspeakers.com.
Cover designed by Jessica Handelman
Interior designed by Mike Rosamilia
The text of this book was set in ITC Berkeley Oldstyle.
Manufactured in the United States of America 0714 OFF
2 4 6 8 10 9 7 5 3 1
Library of Congress Cataloging-in-Publication Data
Malone, Jen.
At your service / by Jen Malone. — First Aladdin MIX edition.
p. cm.
Summary: As the junior concierge at her father's posh hotel, thirteen-year-old Chloe escorts three troublemaking royals on their trip to New York City.
[1. Hotel concierges—Fiction. 2. Hotels, motels, etc.—Fiction. 3. Princes—Fiction. 4. Princesses—Fiction. 5. New York (N.Y.)—Fiction.] I. Title.
PZ7.M29642At 2014
[Fic]—dc23
2014002072
ISBN 978-1-4814-0283-5
ISBN 978-1-4814-0284-2 (eBook)

To John, Jack, Ben, and Caroline,
the best hug givers I know

Acknowledgments

Unlike Chloe's lists, mine could include a C *and* a D–Z yet still not have enough letters to name all the ways Annie Berger is, quite simply, the very best editor a girl could ask for. Her collaborative spirit made the entire experience a complete joy. Plus, she let me flail and squeal over how amazing this "my book is for real actually getting published" stuff is and never laughed at me (or at least not too loudly).

I'd also like to thank the entire team at Aladdin, especially Jessica Handelman and Annabelle Metayer for a perfectly adorable (and *purple!*) cover, Katherine Devendorf for making these pages look so perfect, the marketing duo of Emma Sector and Carolyn Swerdloff for all their hard work, and Amy Cloud for stepping in so seamlessly.

Special thanks to Holly Root, who lives up to her rockstar agent reputation at every turn and sometimes sends me pictures of yawning tigers. I love her equally for both.

My name may be on the cover, but there is a slew of people who can lay claim to aspects of this book. A ginormous-doesn't-cover-it thank you to the most astute critique partners out there: Dee Romito, Gail Nall, Alison Cherry, and Melanie Conklin. Your green highlighters make me giggle, your notes make me better, and your cheerleading makes this all extra-special. Another shout-out to my lovely beta readers: Nicola Call (who checked my "British" like the native she is), Hay Farris (even her in-text notes are hilarious), and Marieke Nijkamp (for mad Guitar Guy love).

I owe a debt of gratitude to the people who took time away from their jobs to explain them in minute detail to me: David Sargent, concierge extraordinaire at Boston's Revere Hotel (and his niece Paisley for letting me borrow her name) and Mary Cavet, who had me drooling with envy while walking me through a Rockettes rehearsal. Guys, she's a Rockette. Enough said.

In an industry that could be so cutthroat, the fact that everyone in our kid-lit community gives time, energy, knowledge, and genuine good wishes to help others' dreams come true restores my faith in humanity every day and makes my "job" so much more meaningful! Special shout-out to my MG Betareaders, my SCBWI critique groups, Katherine Bush, and my OneFourKidLit friends.

Closer to home, I have to thank my mom and dad for passing on their love of words in a hundred little ways, from tracing letters on my back at naptime, to teaching me to read with flash cards, to never getting on my case for having my head buried in a book 24/7. And to Kristen, for providing inspiration for every bratty little sister I write. Who knew she'd grow up to be way cooler than I am?

Giant smooches to Jack, Ben, and Caroline: no matter how much fun it gets in my imaginary world, the fact that they exist in my real one is my very favorite thing about life.

(Almost) last on the list, but first in my heart: my husband, John. That he spent a good chunk of an NYC business trip photographing every penny machine in this book (shh . . . don't tell his boss) is only one of a million billion reasons he's the best thing I ever encountered on a highway. I wouldn't want anyone else by my side. SHMILY.

And to my readers (especially you *girls*!): thank you so much for reading. Never stop, and always remember: go big or go home!

Chapter One

O h. Holy. Yikes.

Pygmy elephants sound like they'd be adorable, but when they look ready to charge at you? Mmm . . . not so much.

I crouch low in the tall African grasses, the stalks tickling my bare calves below my skirt, and *try* to hold as still as possible. News flash: not super easy in heels. Even the really short kind, which is all Dad lets me wear. The narrow beam from my flashlight wobbles, and I have to clamp one hand on top of the other to steady it.

"Almost there," comes Professor Mosley's muffled voice. "Aim the light a tad bit higher, Chloe. Something's . . . ooph! . . . stuck here."

I point the light near the face of the motionless tribesman, not particularly wanting to linger on the elaborately painted designs covering his bare chest or on the spear in his hand, poised to release. Let's not discuss the skimpiness of his clothing (if you can even call a loincloth "clothing"). Eww.

"Aaaaaand . . . got it. Goodness, this is frightfully awkward. I might need a hand with this." Professor Mosley, the museum curator, gestures with a chin jerk for me to move beside him in the glassed-in exhibit as he struggles with the decorated headdress of an eighteenth-century African Irigwe dodo dancer.

"I have to admit, this is not precisely what I had in mind for my Friday night," he says with a sigh, in a British accent that might sound snooty if you didn't know he's actually really nice.

I stretch my arms up to help him lower the ceremonial costume from the head of the mannequin tribesman, careful not to disturb any of the banana fronds along its edges.

"Kinda heard that one before, Professor . . . ," I grunt as the weight of the headdress hits me. How on earth did people wear these things?

We tiptoe around the grass hut toward the exit at the back of the glass case, which is:

At Your Service

A. Again, not so easy in heels. Even mini ones.

B. Even less easy carrying something that probably weighs more than the remarkably realistic-looking elephant we have to maneuver past.

C. No C, actually. But lists with only A and B look sort of lonely.

A night guard nods to us as we step out. He hangs an EXHIBIT CLOSED sign on the velvet ropes he'd set up along the front of the display.

Professor Mosley tells him, "No need for concern, we'll have the display sorted out before opening time tomorrow."

"You're the boss, sir," the guard says.

"And aren't I cursing that fact tonight," Professor Mosley mutters, then turns to me. "Only for your father, young lady. Truly, I cannot imagine anyone else I would open the museum for after closing time to sneak out an African headdress. And just so that one of your hotel guests can have an impromptu wedding ceremony performed in traditional garb."

It's true, people will do practically anything for my dad. It probably also doesn't hurt that Professor Mosley knows Dad will be sure to send an insane number of guests to visit the American Museum of Natural History's new exhibit this week. Concierges rely on favors, but we always try to return them quickly.

I say "we," but really it's Dad who's the concierge. For now, at least. Someday my name will be whispered in the same worshiping tones he commands from everyone in the hotel industry. At least I hope.

If you've ever stayed in a fancy hotel, you've probably seen a concierge, tucked away at a podium or in an alcove to the side of the check-in desk. If your parents needed theater tickets or a dinner reservation or something just a tiny bit weirder, like an incubator to keep the peacock eggs they're traveling with warm, they probably went straight to the concierge. And if he (or she) was anything like my dad, he (or she!) got it for them. Even the incubator. Dad likes to say there's no such thing as an outrageous request.

I don't know about *that*, since I've heard guests ask for some pretty crazy things (hello, if you need to sleep in a hyperbaric chamber, you should probably just stay home), but I do know Dad never disappoints.

"At your service," he says with a smile to every guest who approaches him at the St. Michèle, the very best (in my honest opinion) hotel in New York City.

At Your Service

Basically, if my dad can't get it for you, it doesn't exist.

At the moment I'm sort of wishing this headdress didn't exist, because it's really awkward to carry. It's taking all my effort to keep it from scraping the floor and that's *with* Professor Mosley holding up his end and most of the middle part.

We maneuver our borrowed treasure down the deserted, dimly lit hallways of the museum, our footsteps echoing. I'm glad when Professor Mosley starts making conversation. It helps take my mind off the fact that if I drop this, I've pretty much destroyed a priceless and irreplaceable museum artifact, along with any hopes of following in Dad's footsteps.

"Well, regardless of the circumstances, it's always delightful to see you, Chloe. Not only are you the spitting image of your father, but you're just like him when it comes to handling the impossible."

Okay, so there are a whole bunch of things wrong with what he just said. First, even in his baby pictures, my dad never had the little cluster of freckles that cover the top of my nose and cheeks (which I either love or hate, mostly depending on the day), and second, Dad's hair is dark brown, like an éclair from La Maison du Chocolat on Madison Avenue, while mine is more the blondish color of the wet sand at Rockaway Beach. Plus PLUS, mine's wavy, not straight, *and* I wear glasses.

But the part about my skills being like his makes me squirm, half out of embarrassment and half out of pride. I know they're not. Yet. But they will be if I have anything to say in the matter. I can't think of any job that is more challenging but also totally rewarding. Making people happy—even if it's only for the length of their vacation—is like having a superpower.

Professor Mosley lets loose with a giant sigh as we shuffle along. "Truly, I am going to need a stiff brandy by the time this night is over. Tell me, do they let eleven-year-olds into bars these days?"

"I'm almost thirteen, but no, sir. It's strictly Shirley Temples for me."

He grunts, shifting the weight of the headdress slightly. I have to do a quick sashay-step to avoid tripping. I really don't envy the bride who's going to have this thing on her head. Now I get why the ceremony is seated.

Professor Mosley catches his breath for a second, then asks, "So, this wedding . . . Am I to understand this guest already had a million-dollar church ceremony a few days ago? Was that one not elaborate enough?"

"Apparently the bride's mother decided at the last minute she couldn't give her blessing to the marriage until a traditional tribal wedding is performed. Since the tribe is in

At Your Service

Nigeria and we're in Manhattan, we're improvising. All *we* want at this point is for the bride to stop crying and start enjoying her honeymoon. The other guests are starting to complain about the sobbing noises."

"And your dear father was able to find a Nigerian fellow in New York who knows the ritual? Amazing!"

I can see the door—and salvation—steps away. Yahoo. My fingers cramp a little, and I try to wiggle them without losing my grip.

"Dad's still back at the hotel working out the details, but he's found someone."

Pushing the emergency-exit door open with his back, Professor Mosley guides us down a ramp and over to a limousine parked behind the loading dock. My driver, Bill (well, really the Hotel St. Michèle's driver, on loan for official hotel business), is waiting with the car doors open. He rushes over to take the weight off my hands. Gotta love Bill. Together the two men slide the headdress gingerly across the backseat of the limo.

When it's safely in place, I finally let all the air out of my lungs.

Reaching into the front seat for my sequined purse, I pull out a neatly numbered to-do list and a pencil topped with a fluffy yellow pom-pom that perfectly matches my canary-colored sweater set. It's kind of a thing with me. Every day I pick out the pen that matches my outfit and tuck it into my purse. This is the kind of attention to details that hotel staffers at ultrafancy hotels need to be very good at, so I figure I should get in the habit as soon as possible.

I consult my list. Okay, so all we need now is some face paint to stand in for colored clay, a wooden drum, and a bunch of noise-canceling headphones for the guests in the adjoining rooms. Easy peasy.

I make a million and twelve promises to the professor that I will guard the headdress with my very life, then scoot into the front seat next to Bill.

"Where to, Sunshine?" he asks.

As Bill slides the limousine into a swarm of yellow taxi-cabs, I unlock my smartphone and begin punching buttons, working off a list of numbers for instrument rental shops on the Upper West Side.

Yup, just another day in the life of a concierge at New York City's finest hotel (well, technically in the life of the concierge's daughter, but still . . .). And if things continue to go this awesomely, I'm one step closer to earning my own spot among the legends in the hotel biz.

Chapter Two

So it's been four days since the world's most cosmopolitan tribal wedding ceremony, and the drumbeats are still thumping around in my head, but otherwise, things are mostly getting back to normal. Or as normal as it gets when you live at the Hotel St. Michèle. Which means, not that normal at all.

But seriously cool.

When Mom died five years ago, Dad wanted a change of scenery, so he finally let himself be stolen away from his old hotel by the competition. But not before he worked out a sweet deal that included our apartment "on premises." That way he could keep an eye on me while he worked. Did I mention Dad's really good at negotiating?

Jen Malone

Now he gets to offer "service with a smile" to all the posh guests, and *I* get to have a whole hotel for a backyard. Plus, I can help Dad at work any time I want. Since the hotel maids clean our living quarters, Dad lets me count helping him out with concierge stuff as my chores. Which totally works for me because:

A. I don't have to make my bed or empty my trash or even hang up my towels if I don't want to (except I usually do anyway, because I'm not a total slob; also, I don't want to make extra work for Housekeeping, since they always sneak me the tiny bubble-bath bottles from the maid's cart).

B. I can soak up everything Dad does, the way Chef's biscotti soak up the hot melted chocolate he sends me after school. Plus, the more I learn from Dad, the more often he'll call me his "Capable Chloe."

C. Yup. Still no C.

My friends use a different nickname than Capable Chloe. They call me Eloise, after the children's book about that girl

At Your Service

who lives at the Plaza. Of course, just because I live in a hotel doesn't mean I can get away with any of the stuff Eloise* does in the book. Mostly because she's the daughter of a guest (and guests are always, always, ALWAYS right) and I'm the daughter of an employee. *Big* difference.

The St. Michèle is no Plaza Hotel, though.

It's way better.

When you put your hand on the shiny brass handle and spin yourself through the sparkling glass revolving doors, all the honking and jackhammering and subway-brake screeching noises of the city whoosh away and you step inside a fairy tale. Everything in it is marbled and golden and mirrored and wrapped in two-thousand-thread-count Egyptian cotton. If you're lucky enough to stay at the St. Michèle, you're pretty lucky in general. Because you're also probably pretty rich.

Or you're the daughter of the concierge.

Most days there's nowhere I'd rather be than hanging around the hotel. Today I'm not so sure, judging from the look on Dad's face as he lowers the phone from his ear.

---

* Speaking of Eloise, she might have thought the Plaza was the only hotel in New York City that let you have a turtle, but she was so, so wrong. We've totally had turtles here. And dogs, cats, ferrets, hamsters, teapot pigs, goats (once), and chinchillas. Pretty much the only New York City animal you will not *ever* find in the St. Michèle is a rat.

It's like he's just seen a ghost, only our hotel isn't one of those haunted ones. Guests sometimes say they hear strange noises coming from the air vent in room 1421, but I happen to know for a fact that the vent in that room leads directly to a supply closet where Bobby, one of the busboys, likes to sneak off to nap. And that guy can SNORE!

"What's up, Dad?"

His hand shakes slightly as he places the phone on the cradle, and he has a faraway look in his eyes. Dad is *never* frazzled, so this can only mean one thing.

Uh-oh.

"La . . . La . . . LaFou," he finally manages.

This is bad.

Really, really bad. Sound-the-alarm bad.

Not all rich people are pains in the butt; in fact, most of our guests are super friendly. But the LaFous could write a whole book about how to be the worst hotel guests since the beginning of time (or whenever hotels first started anyway). I can see it now:

Chapter 1: Never be satisfied with anything anyone tries to do for you, *ever*.

Chapter 2: Remember, all complaints sound much better when screamed at an insanely loud volume.

At Your Service

Chapters 3–23: Repeat.

"How much time do we have to prepare?" I ask Dad. But before the word "prepare" is finished leaving my mouth, I glance out the window and spy a head full of fat curls bouncing along on top of a small round body. Then the whole package comes whirling through the revolving door. Her nose is so far in the air, I'm not sure how she's managing to walk a straight line. I'm guessing part of the reason it's up there is to avoid the cloud of perfume that's practically visible around her, like the dirt bomb that surrounds Pigpen. What little kid wears perfume, anyway?

Marie "The Terror" LaFou is four foot zero of sheer spoiled brat.

A minute later her super-skinny mother pushes into the lobby, snagging her long pearl necklace on the door handle and tripping over the hem of her floor-length dress. A businessman by the coffee cart slaps a hand over his eye, having just been temporarily blinded by the beams of light shooting off Madame LaFou's bazillion-carat ruby ring.

Marie's father ambles in behind them like he owns the place. Bellhops and doormen, fingers crossed for a ginormous tip, follow behind in formation, drooling like little kids lining up at an ice cream truck.

The procession makes its way to the front desk, but just before they reach it, Monsieur LaFou veers off to Dad's concierge podium.

Here we gooooooooo. . . .

"Meetch-ell, my good man. 'Ow have you bean?" His French accent always cracks me up. He doesn't wait for Dad to answer before blustering on. "Sorry for zee short no-teece." (Yeah, right.) "It eez Mademoiselle Marie's ninezzz bearzday zees monzzz—can you beleeve eet?—and we 'ave already 'ad parties een Pariz and a zleepover for 'er zeventy-two clozeest friendz on zee yacht in zee South of Franz. But, when I ask *ma petite princesse* what she wantz her next prezent to be, do you know what she ask for? Do you?"

Hmm . . . a pink chimpanzee with a diamond collar to fetch her bonbons and café au laits?

Once again he continues talking before my father's lips have even had time to part. "Well, Meetch-ell, I shall tell you. She zaid, '*Papa*, I want zee bezt bearzday week ever . . . in New York Zity.' Of course, we hopped right on our plane and 'ere we are."

Did he just say WEEK??!!!

Dad swallows visibly. He fixes his smile into place and says, "Of course, sir. I'm at your service."

Oh, *this* is gonna be interesting.

Chapter Three

It's Day Three of the French Invasion and things are not looking up.

Way late last night I overheard Dad on the phone in his bedroom, trying to assure Monsieur LaFou that he would do everything in his power to please young Marie, but could they at least agree that a unicorn would be quite impossible to track down, given the fact that unicorns DO NOT ACTUALLY EXIST.

Like I said before, if it *exists*, Dad can get it.

Poor Dad. He so doesn't deserve this. He should get a special award at the next Les Clefs d'Or conference. They're this super-elite organization for concierges, and you have to be the best of the best to wear their golden-key membership pin. Some day . . .

Anyway, I've been trying to help by staying out of Dad's way as much as possible, which really isn't so much a problem for me. It's not hard to stay entertained at the St. Michèle.

After school I toss my backpack on my bed and swap out my school uniform for a black (hello, I'm a New Yorker, and black is practically a residency requirement) peasant blouse and black (*native* New Yorker here) trouser pants. I straighten my glasses, then add a black fine-tip pen to my purse, which I sling across my chest so it rests flat against my hip. Professional, yet ready for any task, exactly like a hotel staffer should look.

The door clicks shut behind me, and I head immediately down to the loading docks, where there's bound to be some action. Right away I spot Mercy from Housekeeping. She's busy stacking case upon case of Coke cans onto a rolling luggage cart.

"What's all this?" I ask.

"We've got a whole slew of Coca-Cola people staying here tomorrow for their annual sales meeting. I'm going to swap out all the Pepsi cans in the minibars of their rooms with these Coke cans. Wanna help?"

Voilà! Afternoon solved. Mercy wears a little radio clipped to her waistband, and whenever she's not in earshot of any guests, she cranks it up and we sing along. Really, really badly. I double adore hanging with Mercy.

Everything is perfect until, in the middle of us taking advantage of a deserted hallway to add in some choreographed dance moves, Mr. Whilpers rounds the corner. Mr. Whilpers is my evil nemesis, a.k.a. the hotel manager, a.k.a. the boss of everyone in the hotel (except for the owner). He has a handlebar mustache (yes, for real) that he spends all day smoothing and combing. Although he should be paying more attention to his eyebrows, because they're fuzzier than the roller on the shoe-shine machine in our lobby. His face is usually all puffy with importance and blotchy red, but when he spots me, he turns an even deeper shade, like a turnip.

This is because he hates me. Not just me, but all kids. Well, but most especially me, because my dad's super-duper negotiating skills scored us the apartment that *should* have gone to Mr. Whilpers, and now he has to take the subway home to Queens every night.

"Chloe Turner! What have I told you about disturbing the staff during work hours?"

"Um, not to do it?" I offer.

"Precisely. And yet, you somehow manage to get underfoot everywhere I look. Care to explain?"

"Well, Mr. Whimpers—er, Whilpers—um, sir . . . I was assisting Mercy with her workload, and because of my help she managed to finish so far ahead of schedule we determined she had a few spare minutes to work in a bit of exercise. Knowing how important the physical health of your employees is to you, of course, sir, I never imagined this would be something you could possibly object to."

Mr. Whilpers closes his eyes while he takes a very, very deep breath (which gives Mercy the opportunity to fist-bump me). Then he exhales so forcefully his mustache blows up from the breeze.

"I would encourage my staff to address their workout sessions in private spaces and, preferably, on their own time. As for you, Chloe, I think you could find somewhere else to be, yes?"

I salute him (mostly because I know he HATES when I do that) and wave a cheery good-bye to Mercy.

It's fine. I'm starting to lose my voice from the singing, and, after staring at all that candy in the minibars, my stomach is rumbling. I head to the employee cafeteria and wolf down an early dinner of lasagna, join a quick game of gin rummy with two doormen on a break, and then swing by the lobby. I don't want to bother Dad, but I do want to check in, in case maybe he needs my help after all.

At Your Service

Dad is frowning at the phone and saying a whole lot of "Yes, sir." And "I understand perfectly, sir." And "I do apologize, sir."

Three guesses who Dad is talking to.

"Monsieur LaFooey?" I ask when Dad hangs up.

"Don't ever let Monsieur LaFou hear you call him that! But . . . yes." Dad's shoulders slump underneath his fancy suit.

"Lemme guess. Pool too cold? Too hot? Shower pressure too high? Too low? Bed too hard? Too soft? Room too loud? Too drafty? Too blue? Not blue enough?"

"Yes, to all of those things. But this time it was about Marie. She's still not happy with her birthday week activities. And the thing is, I've exhausted most of my contacts getting her the best tables for lunch and dinner at the finest restaurants, the swankiest tickets to the opera, and even a tour of MoMA led by the in-house restoration artist. Nothing pleases that girl."

"No offense, Dad, but kids aren't just miniature adults. She'd probably rather admire Kit or MacKenzie or one of the other American Girls instead of a Warhol at MoMA."

"I always see kids at the Museum of Modern Art!"

"Well, yeah, but do they look happy . . . or tortured? I mean, I'm sure some kids love the art museum. I actually didn't mind it *that* much on our last school field trip. But

Marie seems like she'd be a little more wrapped up in shopping. What about Nintendo World in Rockefeller Center? There's a LEGO store there too."

"I didn't start this gig yesterday, Chlo. I've sent her to those spots already. I know she's a LaFou, but I'm not so sure she likes to shop. Her parents own the biggest department store in Paris, so maybe she gets to do enough of that at home? I never thought I'd say this, but this girl just may have bested me. I'm at the end of my rope here."

Huh. Dad at the end of his rope? I didn't think his particular rope had an end. *Then again* . . . My brain begins to whir. Maybe this could be exactly the opening I've been looking for to take my own concierge dreams to the next level.

"Um, Daddy?" I give him my sweetest, dimpled smile. "What if *I* gave it a try?"

"Hmm?" Dad is only half listening, drumming his fingers on the podium.

"What if I came up with an itinerary for Marie?"

Dad looks up, his eyebrows high. "Sweets, I'm not sure that's a good idea. It's not that I don't trust you to handle yourself professionally. Everything you did with that wedding last weekend sure proved it. In all honestly, if it were anyone other than the LaFous . . ."

At Your Service

"Please, Dad, I *know* I could do it." I bounce a little on my toes and pull my glasses down the bridge of my nose, so he can see the longing, er, the sincerity in my eyes.

"I . . ."

"Oh, Dad, pleeeeeeeeeease?"

"How about this? Why don't you come up with some ideas and we'll go from there, okay? But just ideas, nothing more. Hear me?"

"Thank you, Daddy. Thankyouthankyouthankyou! You won't be sorry!"

Um, I'm pretty sure.

Chapter Four

I leave before Dad has time to reconsider, and settle myself into the wooden-benched phone booth outside of the ladies' lounge. Barely anyone uses a pay phone these days, so it's the perfect thinking spot.

Okay. Ideas.

Ideas, ideas, ideas.

How do I find out what Marie likes without Dad getting upset that I'm meddling?

I scroll through my mental images of Marie from past visits. There was the time she was six, when they came for Christmas. That was the year she crashed into Patrick from Room Service as he was making his way down the hallway with a glass of red wine he was delivering. When they collided, the wine spilled all over Marie's white poufy dress, and she screamed so loudly that more than one guest called 911 from his room. Then her parents threatened to sue the hotel for serving their underage daughter alcohol, since some wine inadvertently landed in her mouth as she screeched. Even three years later the hotel puts Patrick on paid leave the minute the LaFous check in.

So, nothing with any potential spill factor involved.

There was the time she was seven and insisted she could only sleep in a loft, and the hotel had to send Terrence from Maintenance to construct a temporary bunk six feet off the ground.

That was special.

Last year, when she was eight, she requested a dolphin be flown in to swim with her in the hotel pool. But we eventually got out of that one because the Board of Health wouldn't permit it.

Okay, she likes screeching, sleeping up high, and swimming with marine animals. This isn't exactly giving me much to go on. What I need is a little recon. How can I get Marie to give me the goods without letting her in on my plans and making Dad upset that I started working the job without his okay?

I need a more comfortable thinking spot, so I take the elevator up to the third floor and head back to my apartment.

You know that expression "Home is where the heart is"? Well, in my case, it actually is. Like, literally. Any part of the hotel that guests don't see is called the heart of the house. I live in the manager's quarters, just behind the sales offices. It might not be as sparkly as the guests' rooms, but it's way, way cozier.

Our apartment is really three hotel rooms linked together. One is our living room, with a kitchenette. We eat most of our meals in the employee cafeteria, so we don't need much in the way of cooking gear. Then Dad has one bedroom and I have the other. Dad's is still decorated with the same boring boat paintings and silk drapes as every other room in this place, but he let me get a little more creative with mine. He even traded Rolling Stones concert tickets a guest changed his mind about to Terrence in exchange for him painting my room lamplight yellow.

I sprawl out on my patchwork quilt and push play on my iPod. Mom got me hooked on coffeehouse acoustic covers when I was little, and even though it's fun to listen to the more upbeat stuff with my friends (and Mercy), I hardly ever listen to anything else when I'm alone now.

At Your Service

It makes me feel like Mom's still around, when really all I have left of her is—

Wait a minute!

I jump down and drop to my knees. Sticking my head under the dust ruffle, I stretch my arm out and grab a box from underneath my bed. I flip the top off and rifle through it until I find what I'm looking for. Voilà: Mom's slam book.

When Mom was my age, she and her friends had a notebook they passed around. Along the top of every page was a question: How old are you? What's your favorite color? What's your favorite movie? Have you ever kissed a boy? And then under each question on each page was a list of numbers.

How it worked was that you gave it to your friends and assigned them a number. Then the whole way through the book, they answered every question on the number line they were assigned. In her book, Mom was number one (duh, since it was *her* book). By flipping the pages and reading all the answers under the number one, I can tell you that twelve-year-old Mom loved the color red but hated beets. Her favorite movie was *Grease 2*, and her favorite book was *Anne of Green Gables*. Her favorite song was Rob Base and DJ E-Z Rock's "It Takes Two." And, unlike me, she'd already kissed one boy: Scott Bell. But then she must have been embarrassed about it, because she crossed out his name a bunch of times, so it was really hard to read.

This could be the *perfect* way to learn everything I need to about Marie without her getting suspicious. Like a survey, only better.

Now for some supplies and major backup, in the form of my best friend, Paisley.

I send her a quick text, wait for the reply, then race down to the lobby. I force myself to slow once I come into sight of the concierge podium.

I'm casual. I'm breezy. Nothing special going on here.

"Hi, Dad. So . . . you know how tomorrow's a half day at school?"

"Hmm? Oh, okay. I have to work at two o'clock tomorrow, sweets. Sorry."

"No problem. But I was just thinking. Yes, tonight's a school night, but not *technically* a school night since nothing critical ever happens on a half day. So it's like a quasi school night, ya know?"

Dad nods his head at a guest walking by. "Enjoy your afternoon, sir." He continues to keep eagle eyes out for guests as he rests his hands on his podium. "Where are you going with this, Chlo?"

At Your Service

"Can Paisley spend the night? Pleeeeeease, Dad? I have a *great* idea for this thing with Marie and I really need Pay's help."

Dad sighs. I know him well enough; sighs like that equal S-U-C-C-E-S-S. "Thank you, Daddy!"

I bounce away from him and head straight to the check-in desk. There aren't any guests waiting, so I step up to the counter and prop my elbows on it.

"Hey, Annalise. Have the rooms been flipped* yet?"

"Hey, Chloe. What's shaking? We're all flipped except for the ones we're leaving dropped tonight," she answers. This is *exactly* what I was hoping she'd say. When hotels aren't sold out, they sometimes skip (or drop) cleaning rooms so they can have fewer maids on a shift.

"Can I have one?" I ask.

"Sleepover time?" Annalise knows me well. I nod.

"Need adjoining rooms? How many girls are you having this time?" I'm pretty famous at school for my sleepovers, and I've hosted some epic ones for my friends. When we had a cancellation last summer, Dad even let us use the penthouse

---

* That's hotel speak. It just means all the rooms have been cleaned and are ready for new guests.

so we could have an outdoor sleepover on the ginormous balcony, *and* he sent the piano player from our lounge to serenade us on the baby grand up there.

"Just one. A room with a king bed will be perfect."

Annalise types away on her computer, then hands me a stack of key cards. "These rooms are all empty. Check 'em out, see which one is cleanest, and let me know which one you pick, okay?"

I squeal my thanks and zoom back to the elevators. I've spent a *ton* of time helping Mercy and my other friends in Housekeeping turn rooms, and I can flip a suite in no time flat. I veto the first one because it smells like pizza, but the next one I check looks like it was barely slept in the night before. I bump into Mercy in the housekeeping closet, and with her help the bed is changed, the towels swapped out, and the room vacuumed in less than fifteen minutes. She even volunteers to do the toilet *and* the bathtub since I'd helped her with the Coke cans.

I return to the lobby, hand the rest of the key cards back to Annalise, and let Dad know I'm headed out to the Duane Reade drugstore on the corner to buy a new composition notebook and more colored pens. Then I return to my apartment, grab my pj's and toiletries bag, and text Paisley our room number.

At Your Service

Ten minutes later I meet her in our own private hotel room.

"Unless there's something really awesome on the in-room movie selection this time, I brought entertainment."

She holds up a stack of DVDs, all musicals. Pay and I are total Broadway-baby wannabes, even though neither of us can sing a note on key.

"Movie marathon!" I squeal. "I totally have a project for us later, but should we hot tub first or sauna?"

Sleepovers are the best. Sleepovers when you live in a hotel? Best of the best.

We hit the hot tub and sauna in the spa, then head back to our room, put on the giant fluffy robes, and order room service dinner. Chef surprises us by sending up a make-your-own-ice-cream-sundae cart for dessert. When we finally settle down on the edge of the giant Jacuzzi bathtub, with our feet in gurgling water, we're ready to get started on my slam book idea.

"I love this! We should totally do one for school, too. Don't you think it would be fun to see everyone's answers?" Pay asks. "I'm dying to know who Lily is crushing on. Everyone says Tyler, but I *swear* she likes Miles."

"One step ahead of you. I bought two notebooks." I hold up the spare and Pay smiles.

"Always prepared, Chlo."

I smile back. "That's sort of my thing, right?"

We spend the next half hour switching up pen colors and trying to alter our handwriting so we can create an authentic-looking fake slam book for Marie. When we finish, it's a masterpiece, if we do say so ourselves.

"This is perfect. It *has* to work," Pay says.

"I know. I'm so excited I don't think I'll be able to sleep. Do you think we should try to do it tonight?"

Pay pulls her feet from the tub and peeks over at the clock. "It's only eight thirty. She's probably still up, don't you think?"

We get dressed as fast as we can, and I pull my hair into a neat ponytail and slap on lip gloss from my toiletry kit. If we're going to be interacting with a guest, I have to look professional. I know Dad doesn't want me doing anything without his permission, so we head down to the lobby first to fill him in.

Except the elevator stops on the second floor and I happen to spot a very distraught-looking sales manager mopping sweat off her brow as she leaves the Hudson, one of our conference rooms. I recognize the look in her eyes. Slamming my hand into the elevator doors to keep them from closing, I motion Pay to step out with me.

At Your Service

"Mrs. Hathaway, you don't look so hot. Is it at all possible you have one of our more challenging guests in there? About this tall?" I hold my hand up to my shoulder. "Answers to Marie?"

Mrs. Hathaway's eyes roll to the ceiling. "Please do not say that name in my presence again, Chloe.* Monday cannot get here soon enough."

"So that's a yes, then?"

She sighs. "Yes. She's reserved it to watch a movie in there on our projection screen. Apparently the eighty-inch TV in her room is too miniscule and was causing her to squint."

"Perfect. Thanks!" I place my hand on the door handle of the Hudson and tell Pay to stand guard in the hallway. Dad will just have to accept that Fate got to me before I could get to him.

"You're going in there voluntarily?" Mrs. Hathaway looks astonished.

"It's for a good cause." She doesn't seem convinced, but she puts her hand on my shoulder and looks straight into my eyes, as if she might be preparing to say good-bye forever.

---

* Among other phrases and words I'm not allowed to utter in Mrs. Hathaway's presence: "We're sold out due to the clown convention," "All airports are closed because of the blizzard," and (the most evil word of all) . . . "bedbugs."

"May the luck of the Irish be with you."

I grin and push into the room. Marie is sitting at the head of the enormous wooden table, with her shoes propped up on the antique mahogany.

"Oh, I'm so sorry, I didn't realize anyone was in here. . . ." I pretend to be flustered. Marie gives me one of those looks that starts at my feet and travels slowly to my hair. I force myself to keep a pleasant smile in place.

"You're Marie, right?" I ask.

Her eyes narrow. "Who eez asking?" Her accent is cute, which she could be too . . . if she weren't always frowning.

"Oh, my name is Chloe. I work here at the hotel." Sort of. Hopefully she can't see my fingers crossed behind my back. "I was just looking for Mrs. Hathaway, but I must have missed her. Sorry to have disturbed you."

"*Zut alors!* Make me some popcorn. And zees time I want zee fake movie-theater butter, not zee real stuff."

Okay, I am a professional. A professional would not react to this by calling Marie a name like Bratty McBrattington before storming out. Deep breaths.

She leans farther back in the chair and points the remote at the screen. I've been dismissed. I swivel as if to leave, but as I reach the door, I pretend I've just remembered something. She watches me out of the corner of her eye.

"Um, so, Marie. I was wondering. We keep a special kind of guest book for our VIP guests, and I don't know that you've had a chance to sign it on your other visits. I happen to have it on me, if you'd be interested. If not, it's fine. We just like to get our most special guests in here. I think I have some space for you under Duchess Malika. Oh gosh, I shouldn't have given her identity away. It's all anonymous. Please don't pay any attention to me."

Marie sits up a little straighter when she hears the word "duchess." "Geeve eet 'ere." She sticks out one plump hand, palm up to receive the book.

"Well, if you insist. Here, I have a pen if you need one."

I fork over the slam book and hide my grin. This is too easy.

This is *not* too easy.

Pay and I retreat to our room to read Marie's answers (after sending the hotel driver, Bill, to the AMC Lincoln Square to negotiate some movie-theater butter).

Why didn't I think about how her favorites would all be French things? Favorite movie: *Astérix le Gaulois*. Favorite singer or group: Coeur de Pirate. What good is this going to do me? *Of course* she lists her favorite color as "glitter." Ugh! This doesn't give me much to go on.

We reach the last page, and I prepare to lose all hope.

Secret talent: *I love to kick. I can kick my leg over my head.*

Well, this is interesting. It's not that I'm surprised she loves to kick, I just thought that first sentence would have ended with "people." For another thing, her legs are so short, I would think she'd have difficulty lifting them at all.

Paisley looks at me. "Are you thinking what I'm thinking?"

I clap my hands together. "Bet I am!"

We slam the notebook closed and race down the stairs to the lobby, not even bothering with the elevator. Dad is just finishing with a guest. I tap my foot as I wait for him to deliver his signature line.

"Of course, ma'am, I'm at your service." When the guest moves on, I rush up to the concierge stand.

"Dad. I have the best idea ever. Can you help me?"

To his credit, Dad listens closely as I lay out my plan. He doesn't even seem to react when I tell him I "ran into" Marie on my way to get his permission.

" . . . and then we could . . ." I continue to ramble as Dad's eyes get wide.

"But only if . . ."

At Your Service

Hey, I think he might be on board.

"And that's when I'd . . ."

By the time I finish, he's nodding his head along with me.

"I think that might work. It just might. It's getting late; I'd have to disturb some people at home. . . . You know what? It's worth it."

Paisley and I pace the lobby, while Dad makes phone calls. Ten minutes later he gestures us over.

"Well, Capable Chloe strikes again. It's all set for tomorrow afternoon. There's just one catch. They're insisting someone from the hotel accompany her. I have to be at the concierge desk at two o'clock, so it would have to be . . . well, ah . . . you. You do have a half day, right?"

A whole afternoon in the presence of Miss Frenchy Fancy Pants? I'd have to be crazy.

Or really, really desperate to prove I'm one hundred thousand percent ready for my shot at a concierge desk. I thought I was going to have to wait until I was a lot older, but if I can launch my career now? I can be that much ahead of all my competition when I'm ready to work full-time. Why am I even thinking about this? Not even Marie LaFou can keep me from my shot at my dream. So bring it! I can totally handle a pint-sized brat for one measly afternoon.

"It's no problem, Dad. I'll head straight home after school lets out."

"Great. Though you'll have to hurry a bit. Better yet, I'll send Bill with the car for you. Paisley, too, if she wants. Now, do you think Marie's still up, waiting on that popcorn? I say we pay a visit to *la petite princesse*'s papa and fill him in together."

Chapter Five

Why yes, yes, that *is* a limousine waiting for me at the entrance to my school.

Bill has the car perfectly lined up with the front doors and is leaning against the black stretch in his la-di-da uniform.

"Chloe, you are seriously so lucky. In my next life, I want to come back as you." My friend Camila rearranges the books in her arms as we walk down the steps. Our other friend Maddie grabs her by the elbow after smiling at me.

"It's walking time for us regular people. C'mon, Cam, we'll swing by the ice cream truck on our walk." They wave and I skip down the rest of the steps and allow Bill to open the door for me.

So. Fun.

Bill is just about back to the driver's seat by the time Paisley comes flying out the double doors, her uniform shirt half-untucked and a hole just starting in her tights. Typical Pay. She'd never cut it in the hotel world, but as best friends go, she's five diamonds* all the way.

She stumbles on the last step and basically spills into the car. Once she's settled in her seat, she yanks her backpack strap out of the now-closed car door.

"I'm here. I'm ready. Let me at this French poodle!"

I laugh. "Unfortunately, we basically have to kiss her butt all afternoon. Trust me, having you around will keep me sane, but in front of her we have to be perfect representatives of the Saint Michèle. My reputation, er, I mean *the hotel's* reputation, is on the line."

"Yeah, yeah, I got it. No worries."

But I do worry, a little. This is my shot to prove I can handle grown-up jobs as well as any grown-up can, and no way am I going to mess it up.

---

* Five diamonds is the highest AAA rating hotels can get. It's super hard to score, and fewer than one hundred hotels anywhere have it. Of course we're one of them. But you should see the way the staff goes crazy when they suspect one of the secret raters is checked in. It's best to just leave town on those days, in case it's possible to die from exposure to extreme sucking up.

At Your Service

The minute we pull up to the hotel, Pay and I race to my room, where I nix the blouse she had smooshed into a wrinkled mess in the depths of her backpack. I hand her a perfectly pressed one from my closet, change my outfit too, then steer us back to the lobby.

Where we come to a screeching halt.

Mr. Whilpers is there, deep in conversation with Dad. He's turnip colored again, and Dad has the little pinch line he gets on the top of his nose when he's stressed. This doesn't look good.

Dad gestures me over. "We were just talking about you."

"Oh?" I attempt a casual pose against the podium.

"Mr. Whilpers is concerned that you'll be representing the hotel in an official capacity, when you aren't technically an employee." Dad is usually Mr. Take Charge when it comes to anything related to Mr. Whilpers or his job, but I know he's already worried that he might be throwing me to the wolves by putting Marie in my care. Right now it sounds like all it'll take is one nudge in the other direction, and he'll flip faster than an Olympic diver.

This really isn't good.

"Well, Dad, I can see your point, but I've been helping you out for years and years and *years*, and I think you know you can trust me." I stand perfectly straight and proper.

"Well, yes, of course. You're my Capable Chloe." He turns to Mr. Whilpers and shrugs. "She *is* capable. . . ."

Next to me, Pay nods really hard until I poke her in the side.

Mr. Whilpers opens his droopy walrus mouth. "Of course, I'm sure she's fine behind the scenes. But running errands for you is not the same thing as interacting with a guest on her own."

Dad's smile wavers. Before he can say anything else, I shove my cell phone in his face. I have the screen open to a picture from last week's wedding ceremony/ritual thingy. I'm standing with my arm around the bride, posing with the wooden pipe she's just thrown me.

Yeah, that sounds weird. But here's the thing:

A. Apparently other cultures have the traditional bouquet toss, just with other items. Like wooden pipes.

B. Also apparently, other cultures don't find it strange to toss the bouquet, er, pipe to nearly-thirteen-year-olds.

C. Yeah, still no C.

Anyway, it seems to do the trick with Dad.

He nods his head in a snappy way, which means he's

made up his mind. Mr. Whilpers makes a harrumphing noise and says, "Well, I really do think I'm going to have to take this to Mr. Buttercup."

Of course he'd run off and tattle to the hotel owner. I'm surprised he isn't stuffing his fingers in his ears and waggling them nanny-nanny-boo-boo style. I wait till Dad's head is turned and stick out my tongue at Mr. Wimpy. Two can play this game. His mustache twitches as he glares back at me. Then he pivots and marches across the lobby to his office.

Great. I've got to get us all into that limo before the Whilps gets hold of Mr. Buttercup. With no time to lose I abandon Pay with Dad and race to Marie's suite. I practically drag her out, not paying any attention to her little French protests about my hand on her arm. Her mother barely looks up from her *Vogue* magazine as she blows fake kisses and ta-tas her fingers.

In the elevator Marie crosses her arms and refuses to acknowledge me. Granted, this is no way to start the most important day of my hotel career (so far, of course), but desperate times call for desperate measures. I can suck up to Marie plenty as soon as we pull away from the curb.

Besides, her parents wanted us to keep the specifics of the

outing a surprise, so I'm fully prepared for Marie's mind to be blown, and then all our troubles will be over.

Paisley meets us at the elevator doors. I tug (without making it obvious to anyone watching) Marie across the lobby and use my free arm to catch Pay every time she slips in her borrowed shoes. We're just cramming into the revolving door when I hear my name echo across the lobby.

"Chloe!" Mr. Whilpers is by the elevators and he sounds serious.

Ignoring him, I spin us toward fresh air.

Six steps to the limo. Five. Four. Three. Two.

I shove Marie in. The bellhop opens the hotel door for a guest in a wheelchair, and Mr. Whilpers's voice reaches outside.

"Miss Turner!"

I push Paisley after Marie.

"Hold up, missy!"

I jump in, land in Pay's lap, and reach across Marie to click the lock into place right as Mr. Whilpers appears on the sidewalk.

"Who eeez zat purple-faced man?"

I also ignore Marie. I hit the intercom to talk to Bill, just sliding into the driver's seat.

"Go, Bill, go!"

At Your Service

Paisley and I wave merrily at Mr. Whilpers as the limo screeches from the curb. Like actually screeches. It's possible Bill hates Mr. Wimpy as much as I do.

Marie's head snaps up when I tell Bill, "Radio City Music Hall, please."

"Are we going to zee show? I don't feel like seeeeting all day." Her arms are crossed again. I wonder if they just go there by muscle memory.

"Not exactly," I reply, "You'll see. It's a surprise."

Chapter Six

A few minutes later Bill pulls alongside a non-descript building on Fifty-First Street and deposits us in front of a plain metal door. Marie looks up and down the streetscape, trying to piece together where we've taken her.

"Zees eez not Radio City." Gee thanks, Captain Obvious. Little does she know . . .

"Follow me," I instruct. I'm so excited to see her reaction that I almost can't contain myself. Pay and I exchange a smile as we usher Marie through the door. Inside is every bit as bland as the exterior, with no hint as to what the building holds.

Dad forwarded me his contact's e-mail with very explicit directions, so I know just where to turn in the hallway to land us at the elevator. Marie is still muttering away in French. Even in another language I can tell they probably aren't words a nine-year-old should be using.

When we exit on the seventh floor, we still have to go up two flights of stairs. Here's where we get the first glimpse that this is anything but a typical NYC office building. At the top of the first flight is an open door. Hanging floor to ceiling are rows and rows of matching costumes.

Matching *Rockettes* costumes.

There are the toy-soldier white pants with the red stripe down the sides. Ooh, and the red velvet Santa dresses with the furry snow-white trim. And the brown jackets they wear to dress as reindeer!

"We are zeeing zee Rockettez? You zaid we were not going to zee show."

I smile serenely, like a parent handing a toddler a wrapped present. It's going to be so fun to see her face. "We're not. We're going to a rehearsal. A *Rockettes* rehearsal. A *private* Rockettes rehearsal."

Marie shrugs.

SHRUGS!

Okay, hold up. Look, kid, the freaking Rockettes are letting *you* into their rehearsal so you can watch them high-kick, which is something you claim to love doing yourself, and all you can do is shrug? ERGH!

Paisley grabs my arm and gives me a "forget her" look and a giant smile as I turn us toward another, smaller staircase. At least *she's* excited. And so am I. Granted, musicals are a little more our thing, but the Rockettes are ah-mazing.

The next landing has the hat shop. All the toy-soldier hats hang upside down with their feather plumes waving.

So. Cool.

We follow my e-mail instructions down the long hallway to the rehearsal space. Marie makes the caboose for our little procession. Even before we get there, we can hear "If it feels good, it's probably wrong, girls. Okay, toe the line. Bevel. Now, strut kicks, five, six, seven, eight . . ."

I peek in first, then grab Marie and move her up beside me. She's acting all matter-of-fact, but I'm betting underneath the layers of brat, she's impressed. How could she not be?

About forty girls cluster to one side, either watching the group dancing, chugging from water bottles, or slipping off thin wrap sweaters. In the right corner, to the side of a long stretch of floor-to-ceiling mirrors, are a small piano and a drum crammed against the wall. Jammed tight into the other corner is a table where a man sits making notes. In the very front, with her back to the mirrors, a super-elegant lady dressed in a black flowy tunic sweater, black tights, and black lace-up boots is standing on a small wooden box and calling out to the dancers.

Two of us watch transfixed (the third assumes her standard crossed-arm stance) as the Rockettes move in unison across the floor, kicking and pivoting gracefully. After a minute the man at the table spots us and calls for a break. Forty legs lower as one, and the ramrod-straight line goes all wiggly as dancers drop their form and head for their water.

Wow.

The man makes his way through the sea of dancers. "Hi, girls. I'm the stage manager, Eddie. You must be from the Saint Michèle. Are you Marie?" he asks Paisley, who giggles.

"*I* am Marie." She pushes Pay aside and steps forward. Geez, could her nose stick up any farther?

Eddie looks a little taken aback as he turns to face Marie. I'm sure he expected gushing and maybe even some tears of delight. I know I did.

"Well, Marie. Uh, welcome. We thought maybe you'd like to watch from up front, so you can get a sense for the way the line works."

Marie looks like she's being told the average rainfall in Peru or something equally uninteresting.

"If you zink zat eez best," she says, examining her nails. I truly want to slap her. And I'm not a violent person. Paisley has a panicky look on her face like the one I'm trying to mask on mine. How could all this amazingness still not be amazing enough? When I get back to the hotel, I'm totally in for it. I was so sure this would save the day. Now Wimpy is breathing down my neck, who knows where Mr. Buttercup stands on things, and, worst of all, Dad will be bummed.

I'm sure he won't actually *blame* me or anything, seeing as how he didn't have any better ideas, but I hate to think I let him down. And what does this mean for my goal of being the brightest star in the concierge world if I can't even make one nine-year-old happy in a city as magical as New York?

Well, one thing's for sure. I'm not going down without a fight. The number one rule of concierges everywhere: Remember, it can't hurt to ask.

"Eddie?" I call as he begins leading Marie up front. He turns and I gesture him over.

"I know this is a lot to ask, so please feel free to say no, but this is a very, verrrrrry special guest at our hotel and, well, we're a little desperate to make her stay memorable. She's a bit . . . tough, on the exterior, but inside she's just so excited to be here, ya know?"

At Your Service

Yes, I realize I'm babbling.

"Anyway, what do you think the chances might be of letting her, um, participate in the rehearsal for a little while? Just to give her a taste of what it's really like to be a Rockette. We'd be soooo grateful. I know I will personally tell everyone at my school and, of course, in the hotel, to buy tickets to the show this year. Really. Positively everyone."

Pay is behind me, nodding like one of the Yankee bobbleheads she collects. "Me too."

Eddie hesitates, eyeing Marie's cheetah-patterned jeans. "I . . . She's not really dressed for it."

Oh, Eddie. You clearly have not met me before. The *C* stands for Capable, my dear man. I slide the backpack off my shoulder and hold it up. "I had some dance gear in her size sent to the hotel this morning. You know, just in case."

Eddie looks cornered. "Um, okay, I . . . I guess it would be fine. I'll show you where she can change." He retrieves Marie from her slouching spot against the mirror and returns her to me. Marie's butt print on the glass lingers.

I fill her in and I swear, for one tiny second, I see a flicker of something in those dull shark eyes of hers. She actually looks like she's rushing when we point out the ladies' room.

Score one for me!

Chapter Seven

When we return, the next group of dancers is lining up on the grid lines taped to the floor. Pay and I move aside a jumble of the girls' street shoes and find a spot among the girls sitting this session out. They all smile to welcome us. It's official: I love the Rockettes.

Marie moves directly to the center of the dancers, like she's a queen surrounded by her ladies-in-waiting. I hold my breath.

The glamorous woman who was calling out moves from atop a small box when we first arrived raises her hand, and all talking stops. About eighty pairs of eyes, plus mine and Paisley's, swivel to her. Marie studies her nails again.

At Your Service

"Oh boy. Joyce isn't gonna stand for that. She's all about respect, respect, respect," whispers one of the dancers to me.

Joyce's hair is pulled so tight into a bun that you would think it would yank the corners of her mouth up, but no— her expression looks like she just popped a Sour Patch Kid into her mouth.

She walks—check that, she *glides*—to Marie and stands motionless in front of her until Marie lifts her eyes. Marie looks like she's about to say something snide, but she doesn't. Anyway, I'm putting my money on the choreographer lady in this showdown. She doesn't look like she's ever lost ground to anyone. Of course, Marie did once get our chef to make her gumdrops on his day off. I wouldn't have thought that was possible either.

"Bevel position, please," she instructs.

Marie stares back at her. "What eez zees bevel position?"

"Ah, so you are not a trained dancer. Imagine my surprise. We welcome you here, but I suggest that someone who is not an expert at least learn to take instruction like a professional. Now then. Shoulders back, stand tall, heels together, this knee bent softly, toes pointed, hand on hip. There. Better." The Rockettes assume the same position without prompting.

"Okay, so we will show our guest here a kickline, shall we ladies? Your name is Marie?"

Marie is holding her position so stiffly, she seems hesitant to nod. Ha! So rich, French brat is no match for elegant, intimidating choreographer. Good to know.

"Well, Marie. Let's have some fun. These girls will be practicing for six hours a day, six days a week until opening night. And then they work harder. They will perform sixteen shows a week, up to four shows a day. And do you know why they do this, Marie?"

Marie's head moves back and forth.

"Because they love to dance. Do you love to dance, Marie?"

"I like to kick," she answers, a tiny question mark in her voice.

"Well, good enough. Kick we shall. Girls, toe the line. Marie, I will tell you what we are doing as we do it. Now. See how the girls are lined up with the tallest in the middle and the, well, *less* tall on either end? On stage it will present an optical illusion. They will all look the same height. Theater is magic. Always remember that."

The girls on the floor with me hide their giggles, but the dancers in line hold their positions gracefully, all business.

Joyce continues. "We are very mathematical here. There

are numbered grids on the floor, and each girl has coordinates she follows when she moves. If a dancer steps on her proper lines, she will always be the correct distance from the others. We are all about precision. It wows our audiences. When we toe the line, it means we stand two numbers apart from the girls on either side, with our toes on the line. The fingertips on your right hand will just brush the shoulder blades of the girl on your right, and the fingertips of your left hand will brush the waist of the girl on your left. Understand?"

The dancers assume the position to demonstrate.

"Wait, so they don't actually touch?" I whisper to the dancer next to me.

"Fingertips to fabric," she answers. "That way if one girl loses her balance on a kick, she doesn't take the whole line down with her."

"Cool," Paisley says.

I know today isn't about me, but I'm totally fascinated with everything I'm learning and seeing. Pay and I keep poking each other, letting our elbows speak for us instead of shouting, "Can you even believe we're here?" like we want to.

Joyce physically maneuvers Marie into a spot at the end of the line.

"We'll begin with strut kicks. Marie, lift your right knee

up so your toes are level with your left knee. Now kick straight out."

Marie does this easily. I'm a little impressed. Joyce gives a smile, and the one Marie answers her with is so unexpected it's as shocking as when it snows overnight and I wake up to a totally silent city.

Holy cow. We did it. We did it. We did it! We got Marie LaFou to smile. I want to call the Channel Seven TV crew to cover the breaking news.

"Good, now an eye-high. Marie, feet together, kick, feet together, kick, all the way to your eyeballs. Ready—and a five, six, seven, eight . . ."

I'll give her this, the girl definitely wasn't lying about her kicking skills. She can practically touch her nose with her knee when she wants to, and she actually keeps up perfectly with the kickline. Plus she's doing it all with a genuine grin stretching her face. It makes her almost pretty. For once Marie's kicking (minus the "and screaming" part, of course) is actually enjoyable.

The way I'm feeling, I'm fairly sure *I* could kick for the sky at the moment.

Everything's perfect, until the end, when Marie loses her balance on a kick. Her left leg goes all wobbly and her arms spin like a pinwheel, trying to hit the floor before her butt. They don't.

The other girls crowd her to make sure she isn't hurt and I sit stone still, certain she's broken and my career is over before it began.

Luckily, she struggles to her feet. Her legs shake a little, and for a second I think she's going back down, but she recovers. Whew. No permanent damage done. Although she does look like she might be about to stomp her foot or—please no—blame one of the Rockettes for tripping her. Joyce is quick to take charge.

"This is nothing to worry about. Falls happen. We have an expression here. What is it, girls?" Joyce cups a hand to her ear.

Eighty voices answer the same way they dance—as one. "Go big or go home!"

Marie smiles in appreciation and actually, actually *thanks* every girl she danced with. She even—wait for it—hugs Joyce. And me. And Paisley. I half expect to see flying pigs swooping around when we push out onto Fifty-First Street.

As the limo carries us back to the hotel, I relive the afternoon. *Go big or go home.* I like it. Les Clefs d'Or's "In Service through Friendship" saying is sweet and everything, but I think I just found my own personal concierge motto.

Chapter Eight

Interoffice memo:

Attention: Chloe Turner
From: Xavier Hemsley Buttercup, Hotel Owner

Dear Ms. Turner,

I am pleased to officially welcome you to the staff of the Hotel St. Michèle as junior concierge. As we discussed in our recent meeting, you will be responsible for tending to the needs (and often whims) of our youngest guests. As there are frequent occasions when we do not have children or young adults among our guest roster, your hours will not be regularly scheduled; however, your father has agreed to determine a work routine that will allow you to perform your duties alongside your other responsibilities, such as schoolwork. We're most excited to be the only hotel in New York City to offer this type of personal, peer-to-peer concierge service and hope you will wear the mantle of your role well and with pride.

Sincerely,

Xavier Hemsley Buttercup

Phone message from front desk:

Chloe—Peanut Butter & Co. called @ 11:11 a.m. Heard about your new job & would like to introduce you to their restaurant in hopes you'll recommend it to guests. You + friend invited to dinner at their expense any night this month. Call manager, Steph, at 212-555-1421 to arrange.

Voice mail:

"Hi, Chloe. This is Jack from Macy's department store. I'm Elizabeth Eifler's assistant. Just wanted to let you know, we're all squared away. You'll need to arrive by nine a.m. on Thanksgiving morning, and we've got you and your guest assigned as handlers for the Elf on a Shelf balloon. Wear comfortable shoes—the parade route is two-point-six miles. Oh, and we begin inflating the balloons Wednesday night, so if you wanted to bring your guest over to see that, too, we'd be happy to have you. Your balloon will get inflated on Seventy-Seventh Street between Central Park West and Columbus Avenue, so you can just meet the rest of the handlers there. Call if you have any questions. Thanks! Bye!"

Interoffice memo:

Attention: Bartholomew Whilpers, Hotel Manager
From: Xavier Hemsley Buttercup, Hotel Owner

Bartie,
While I certainly appreciate your taking the time to express your concerns about the recent appointment of Chloe Turner to junior concierge, I'm afraid I do not share them. Furthermore, I fail to see why spotting Miss Turner at the ice machine outside of her apartment in footed Hello Kitty pajamas reflects

poorly on the St. Michèle. For one thing, that hallway is not accessible to hotel guests. For another, even if it was, I'm sure many of our guests would share my opinion that Hello Kitty is, well . . . rather adorable. Thank you for your note and please feel free to reach out to me with any future issues.

Fondly,

Xavier

Comment box on hotel website:

To Whom It May Concern: We stayed at your hotel from January 4th–5th and while the overall service was outstanding, we wanted to single out your young concierge, Chloe, for all of her efforts. When Chloe found out our daughter was having a hard time enjoying herself because she was nervous about her upcoming Mandarin language exam, Chloe arranged for Katie to accompany the hotel sous chef on his grocery shopping trip to Chinatown. Spending a morning fully immersed in the language was exactly what Katie needed to boost her confidence and she was able to relax and enjoy the remainder of our vacation. Of course, she did need three showers after returning from the fish market, in particular, but she claims it was well worth it! We hope Chloe is on your staff for a long time to come, and we'll be booking our next trip at the St. Michèle.

Sincerely,

The Ventresca Family

Phone message from front desk:

Chloe—Lyra Barnes's agent called @ 2:07 p.m. Front-row tickets for the concert will be at will-call & Lyra will be expecting you & your guest backstage after show. Ask for Frank, the stage manager. Call if any issues: 212-555-7557. Autographed headshots will be messengered over later today. (PS: Can I have one?)—Thomas

E-mail:

To: chloeturner@stmichelehotel.com
From: john@tannenbaumtreefarm.com

Chloe,

Although we rarely receive requests for Christmas

trees this many months after the actual holiday, we would be happy to help you create Christmas in February for the grandchildren of your guests. It's too bad the kids weren't able to spend Christmas Day itself with their grandparents, but it sounds like you plan to make this a celebration to remember for them. We can arrange to have someone here to meet you to cut down a suitable tree at 10:00 a.m. on Saturday. And thank you again for the offer to purchase the trees for the hotel lobby from us this year.

Best,

John

Interoffice memo:

Attention: Bartholomew Whilpers, Hotel Manager
From: Xavier Hemsley Buttercup, Hotel Owner

Bartholomew,
I really do wish you would find something other than young Miss Turner's actions to send me memos about. I'm sure guests encountering a choir singing Christmas carols during check-in was unusual, given

that we are months past the holiday; however, my understanding is that the choir was only present for the fifteen-minute window just before and during the check-in of the guests benefiting from this Christmas-in-February treat. I have a hard time believing there were any actual complaints.

Sincerely,

Xavier

PS: It sounds as if you are not a fan of roasted chestnuts, but I personally think arranging for the cart outside the hotel entrance was a brilliant touch on Chloe's part (and I must say I quite enjoyed the ones that were sent up to my offices).

Comment card left in room 1040:

We had a lovely stay and were most impressed with your concierges, particularly the young one. When we mentioned our son loves circuses, we expected her to arrange tickets to Ringling Brothers. We never imagined she would make a whole day of it for him. Taylor can't stop talking about his visit to Frank Bee's Clown Studio and wants to wear his red nose everywhere. Trapeze School New York was another unforgettable memory—flying high over the Hudson River . . . he even spotted the Statue of Liberty while swinging upside down! I can't imagine what could top this trip! We'll be back for sure!

Gift tag from the design studios of Felicity Olson:

Chloe: A little birdie told us you have a big birthday coming up. Welcome to your teenage years! We were told Circle Line was donating a Harbor Lights cruise for your party and thought you might like something special to wear. Please accept this outfit with our compliments, and we look forward to seeing you and your guests in our showroom again soon.

Interoffice memo:

Attention: Bartholomew Whilpers, Hotel Manager
From: Xavier Hemsley Buttercup, Hotel Owner

Mr. Whilpers,
I'm afraid I'm going to have to insist these notes about

Chloe Turner stop. If Chloe claims she had a good reason to escort a baby giraffe through the lobby and out the back to the loading dock, I'm quite certain she did. Kindly direct your attention to other hotel matters and leave Miss Turner be, so that she may continue with the fine job she's doing.

With regards,

Mr. Buttercup

Chapter Nine

Know what's sucky about spending a sunshiny March morning baking cupcakes at Magnolia Bakery at the request of a guest? Absolutely nothing.

"You girls were awesome today. I hope you had fun. Chloe, any time you want to do this again, just give me a call. Hey, enjoy the weather out there. Finally starting to feel like spring around here, huh? Now, how about a few to take home?"

Even though having my arms elbow-deep in batter for hours on end should have me swearing off sweets, no way am I turning down an offer of cupcakes-to-go from the head baker, Hazel.

"Wait, what's in the hummingbird one again?" Emily, my sweet-toothed guest, asks.

"Banana, pineapple, pecan cake with sweet cream-cheese icing," I recite from memory, earning me a thumbs-up from Hazel.

I smile as she places a signature pale green tin with the bakery's storefront logo in my hands and resist the urge to peek at which yummy flavors she's chosen for us. Emily and I give her quick hugs, then slip the aprons over our heads and drop them on the baking table. We scoot around the counter and cut through a long line of customers waiting for their daily fix of buttercream frosting.

"Do you want me to text Bill to pull around, or do you want to scope out a bench and dive into these?" I ask.

"Would you think I was a total pig if I said I couldn't wait to have another one? I know we sampled all morning, but they are sooo addicting."

I smile. If only all guests could be as easy to please as Emily. She's sweeter than the coconut flake cupcake I pass her. "Let's walk up to 30 Rock and grab a bench there. The *Today* show should still be taping, so we can peek inside the windows. And hey, I know you're leaving tonight and we didn't make plans past this morning, but I'm meeting up with some friends from school later at the park and you should definitely tag along. I think you'd love them."

At Your Service

We link arms and walk up Forty-Ninth Street. Second to Christmastime in this part of the city, with the enormous tree in Rockefeller Plaza and the ice skaters and the store windows all decorated, spring is my favorite season in Manhattan. It's like we all hibernated as much as possible through the slushy, gross part of winter, and now the city is coming back to life.

I inhale the smells from the Sabrett's hot dog cart and duck past a tourist holding up a giant IT'S MY BIRTHDAY, PUT ME ON CAMERA sign outside the windows of the studio. Emily and I snag a bench right across the plaza and dig into the cupcake tin one more time.

"Seriously, you're going to have to roll me onto the plane home. I'll be in a major sugar coma." Emily laughs. "Ooh, this is banana and chocolate. Yum! Want the carrot cake one?"

But I don't answer. I'm too busy watching the electronic news ticker that flashes all the top headlines across the top of the NBC studios.

"Chloe? Earth to Chloe?"

But I just point.

Breaking news: King Robert of Somerstein and his family, including Queen Caroline and their three royal children, Prince Alex, 14, Princess Sophie, 12, and Princess Ingrid, 9, to visit NYC next weekend.

Emily squeals. "Ooh. Prince Alex. I've seen his pictures online. He's sooooo cute! I wish my visit was longer. I could hire you to help me stalk him."

"I guess," I answer, preoccupied. I'm not too up-to-date on European royalty and whether they're cute or not, but I do have one burning question.

"I wonder where they're staying?"

I think I've figured that one out.

Clue #1: About six black, unmarked SUVs parked in front of the St. Michèle that are *not* being whisked off by a valet.

Clue #2: An abundance of men in all-black suits roaming the lobby and doing things like picking up the potted ficus tree and peering intently under it.

Clue #3: Mr. Whilpers blotting his sweaty forehead with a napkin-looking thingy he claims his mom made for him. Oh wait, that's not a clue. That happens every day. The man sweats more than a bike messenger headed from the Village to 103rd Street.

Actual Clue #3: My dad blotting *his* forehead with a crisp linen handkerchief. Now *that* is a first for any day the LaFous aren't in town.

The royals are staying HERE.

At Your Service

Oh. Holy. Yikes.

And they're bringing the kids. Where there are kids, there is Chloe.

Double. Holy. Yikes.

Does that mean *I'm* in charge of them?

"Hey, did you hear the news?" Filipe asks. He's a bell-hop, which means he helps people take their luggage to their room. I glance around the lobby for Mr. Whilpers, because it would NOT be good for him to catch me hanging out with Filipe.

Three years ago we got busted big-time for using two luggage carts as scooters in timed races around the fourth floor. We probably wouldn't have gotten in *that* much trouble if I hadn't also tied a bedsheet to the back of mine so I could pull Paisley along behind me. In my defense, I was ten. I'm not so sure what Filipe's defense was.

I lean against the grand piano. "Not officially, but I can guess. Royalty at the Saint Michèle? How cool is that?"

"Very cool. Though Whilpers is having a conniption. He's already ordered new uniforms for all us bellhops and booked the entire staff haircuts in the beauty salon. The salon reserved for *guests*. He's on a tear."

Oooh. I love when Marisa at the salon on our lower level

does my hair. She uses this cucumber-mint styling gel that smells amazing.

Just then I spot Dr. Evil himself rounding a corner and quick as lightning scoot far away from Filipe. If I'm gonna survive the next week of preparation, I'd better keep out of the Whilps's way. I'd say "lie low," but no way am I going to miss being around while we get everything here set. The hotel is normally set for regular VIPs' luxury, so I can't WAIT to see how we ramp it all up for royalty.

Besides, keeping busy with a week of school and hotel prep can only help to keep my mind off what might be in store for a junior concierge expecting a junior prince and princesses.

Chapter Ten

The next Friday afternoon our entire hotel staff lines up to welcome the King and Queen of Somerstein and their royal offspring. Every single inch of the hotel has been polished and spruced and buffed. Pillows have been plumped, pianos have been tuned, carpets have been replaced, a new chandelier was ordered for the penthouse suite, and our weekly fresh-flower order was quadrupled. We are ready.

I'm back and forth between crazy excited and crazy nervous for my "make it or break it" moment. Crazy excited because attending to world-famous visitors can make the career of a concierge faster than our high-speed Wi-Fi signal connects our guests to the Web. Crazy nervous because messing up in any way in front of said world-famous visitors can end the career of a concierge quicker than our head doorman Johnny can hail a cab.

Mr. Whilpers has positioned himself right at the inside edge of the revolving doors, so when the king enters the lobby, he'll land directly in Whimpy's potbelly. Yeah, some welcome. If that happened to me, I'd probably run screaming back to Somerstein.

When the Whilps sees me looking at him, he puts two fingers up to his eyes and then turns them around toward me to mime, *I'm watching you.*

Ooh, scary.

As long as Mr. Buttercup stands by his decision that I can be trusted to take the royal kids around (well, trusted in the sense that their two bodyguards will be a foot away to make sure everyone is safe and secure at all times), I don't see where Mr. Whimps will be watching anything other than me getting in good with the royals.

But I lose my smirk every time I think of the epic task ahead of me. Seriously. Dad says I took to my new job like a duck to water (whatever *that* means), but this is like getting called up to the major leagues. Last night I got a whole "Now that you're thirteen and a teenager, I really think you're ready for this new level of responsibility, and I'm putting my trust in you and counting on you not to let me or the Saint Michèle down" talking-to. Gee, Dad. No pressure or anything. Even though I actually *want* the responsibility, so I can prove myself.

After that, Pay and I stayed up way too late (on a school night, no less, which made today in classes not so much fun) putting the final touches on a dossier of information on each of the royal kids. We figured they were probably too slick to use my patented slam book method of gathering intel, but, luckily, they're celebrities, so getting the dirt on them wasn't all that difficult.

Here's what we found:

Princess Sophie, age twelve:

Sophie is like a paper-doll cutout. In every picture we downloaded, it looks like she has one standard "I've been groomed for life as a princess" pose, and someone has just slapped on different hairstyles and outfits. Tea with the Queen of England? Hair clipped on either side and a sweet rose-colored sundress. Skiing with her father? Jaunty ponytail, stylish goggles propped on her forehead, and perfectly fitted parka and snow pants. Greeting a crowd of well-wishers in the castle courtyard? A green wool suit with a coordinated coat, leather gloves, and a feathered hat that perched at exactly the right angle. She's like Princess Barbie come to life. In one or two of the pictures her smile looks real and not plastic, so I'm crossing fingers *and* toes that she isn't as perfectly perfect as she looks, because how can someone so perfect be normal and fun and nice too?

Princess Ingrid, age nine:

Ingrid is a cutie. She's on the edge of every picture, staring off to the side, like there's always something there she can't wait to check out. But basically, she's your average little kid.

And then we have Prince Alex. Nothing average here.

Prince Alex, age fourteen:

It's *possible* that Alex's dossier is approximately six inches thicker than Ingrid's and Sophie's, but Paisley and I really didn't think it was fair to be forced to choose between pictures of Alex catching waves on the beach or ones of him playing polo. So basically they all went in. Along with the ones of him shopping in Dubai, riding in the back of a convertible in a parade, and taking flying lessons.

I know people always say royals have blue blood, but someone should really do a study about how blue blood might actually be an attractiveness enhancer. The whole family looks like they could pose for a Gap ad. Except they probably don't even know what Gap is, and I'm sure they *definitely* have never set foot in one.

At Your Service

Faint sirens grow more intense and people start picking invisible fuzz off their uniforms and putting a little extra straight in their posture. I half expect Mr. Whilpers to yell, "Ten hut!" and lead us around the lobby in a march.

I catch Mercy's eye and wink. She grins and winks back, once with each eye. This is kind of our thing because we both know that I can only wink with my right eye. Whenever I try to wink with my left one, the whole side of my mouth scrunches up at the same time. Any day I don't have school, I sneak into the maids' morning meeting, where Mr. Whilpers hands out the boards* and gives his daily cheesy pep talk. I always make it my mission to try to crack Mercy up with my winks without letting the Whilps catch on. I like to think it makes hearing his "Remember, everyone, winners never lose and losers never win!" speech for the gazillionth time a little more bearable.

I'm just gearing up for a left-then-right-then-left-eye wink (which I know from experience will make Mercy's whole body shake while she fights a laugh) when two police motorcycles

---

* "The boards" is hotel speak for the list of rooms each maid is assigned to clean that day. It's kind of like a puzzle because every room gets a point value, and bigger rooms are worth more points than smaller ones, so they have to divide it all up so everyone gets the same number of points. If you ask me, picking up someone else's wet towels should count for triple quadruple points.

screech to a halt just past our front door, leaving space behind for the stretch limousine trailing them to line up its back door with the hotel entrance. Right away a doorman rushes over and yanks the limo door open. A whole army of men in black suits has already formed a perimeter around the sidewalk. The photographers they're blocking have to stretch their cameras way up over their heads to take pictures. I bet they end up with a bunch of shots of the fire hydrant, which makes me giggle.

King Robert is super tall, so he has to sort of fold himself out of the limo. Then he turns back to offer his wife a hand.

"Now that man has the manners of a true king," our sales manager, Jean, whispers next to me, and I nod without taking my eyes off the action. They're like something straight out of a Disney movie. The queen places one elegant leg onto the street and allows King Robert to guide her out of the limo. Usually, when it's Bill helping me out of the backseat, he just lets me scoot across the bench and out the door, but if he does give me a hand, he kinda yanks on it to pull me out. This looks more like she glides onto the street. Maybe we'll get to be close friends in the next couple of days and I can ask her how she does that.

The two turn and wave at the gathered crowd before Queen Caroline returns her attention to the other passengers.

At Your Service

She steps back and Ingrid slips out and past her. She's pretty tiny for a nine-year-old, and she goes right to her dad's legs and parks herself behind them.

Sophie is next, and she makes the same graceful exit her mother did. She has a perfectly sweet smile on her face as she does that cupped-hand side-to-side wave thing beauty pageant contestants are always doing. Hmm. That kind of perfect could be pretty easy to hate.

Alex is last. Okay, so he is seriously even cuter in person.* How is that possible? I thought famous people were supposed to be shorter and have bad skin in person. Nope. Alex pretty much looks like he was just delivered from a Choose Your Own Perfect Boy catalog. This is going to be . . . interesting.

I mean, of course, it's not like I could ever fall for him, because that would be seriously the most unprofessional thing ever, and my reputation is way more important than scoring a date with "the hottest thing ever to land on my doorstep who just happens to be a prince."

Way more important.

---

* Like, seriously. He has that kind of messy hair that his mom probably has to sit on her hands not to smooth down all the time, but that everyone else knows looks totally hot. And it's surfer blond. And his eyes are the same navy as the Hudson River just before it storms. And he's tall. And he's got this kind of sideways smile like he knows a secret and he might tell you, but then again he might not. And he's a prince. So there's that.

Definitely.

It's kind of chaotic outside with all of the photographers and the crowds, but the St. Michèle lobby is the quiet haven from the hustle and bustle it always is. Even though the entire staff is lined up and waiting, you could hear a pin drop as the royal family spins through the revolving doors. Although I half expect someone to break out in "Be Our Guest" and start dancing around with the feather dusters.

They enter the lobby all smiles. The whole royal family makes their way past my whole hotel family, and everyone curtsies or bows. Guys just have to duck their heads, but women are supposed to do a small curtsy. I've completed Mr. Whilpers's Bow and Curtsy Boot Camp, and I have it down pat: right foot behind the left heel, bend knees slightly.

The king is first through our lineup, but I'm a teensy-tiny bit more focused on Prince Alex as I slide my left foot behind my right heel. When I glance down, I realize my feet are backward. Whoops. I think Alex might have noticed. I think he might be smirking. Or is he smiling? I can't tell, and now my feet are all jumbled and—

Omigosh, I'm falling!

Ever tried to greet a king and accidentally plunged into his arms instead? No? Huh. I can't say the same. Even though he laughed and helped me upright, you know that expression that's something like how you can't make a first impression twice? That kinda sucks. Because a do-over would be really, really great.

I do NOT think this situation is covered in the Les Clefs d'Or handbook on how to be a world-class concierge.

Chapter Eleven

Redemption time. Even though Dad's and my next meeting with the royals and their security detail is taking place at the rooftop pool, I have on the black suit I wore to meet them earlier. I can't earn my Les Clefs d'Or golden key pin for excellent concierge service until I've been a concierge for three years and am at least twenty-one, but I figure the apple one Dad gave me last Christmas is a close substitute. I pin it to my lapel. There. Nice and official looking.

Too bad my smooth waves are going to frizz the second I set foot in the indoor pool area. No biggie, it's only a prince I'm meeting. Who needs smooth hair for that?

Whoa, Chloe. Stop thinking of him as a prince. Guest. Just a guest. And I have to remember he comes with a set of sisters. I'm pretty sure the itinerary I came up with takes everyone into account, so I just have to remind my brain to do the same.

"Ready, sweets?" Dad asks as we skirt the edge of the pool and I try not to slip on any puddles of water on the tiles. As if falling during a stupid simple curtsy wasn't bad enough.

Dad stops in front of a woman who looks a bit like the grandmother in Little Red Riding Hood. She has her whitish-blond hair piled in a bun on the top of her head and black reading glasses perched on the end of her long, long nose. Her glasses have a fake diamond (OMG—could they be REAL?) chain that loops down on her neck.

"Mr. Turner, lovely to meet you in person. I'm Elise von Guttman, the private secretary of the sovereign."

"A pleasure, Dame von Guttman. And please, call me Mitchell. This is my daughter, Chloe."

"If you are going by Mitchell, then please, just Elise. And Chloe, I have heard so much about you from Mr. Buttercup." She sticks out her hand and I shake it, giving silent thanks that I don't need to curtsy. She seems friendly. Maybe I'm in my head too much about these people being so different just because they have fancy titles. All of a sudden I'm not so scared to meet the actual royals for real (I'm not counting my tumbling act in the lobby as an official introduction). They're just people, after all. How different can we be?

"I would like to review a bit of protocol before the prince and princesses arrive. Would that be acceptable?" Elise smiles her friendly smile, and now I can breathe in the chlorine-scented air no problem. This is going to be fine.

"First of all, should you have the opportunity to speak with the king and queen, you should address them by their formal title, Your Majesty. If you are introducing them to others, it is His Majesty the King Robert and Her Majesty the Queen Caroline of Somerstein. You should only shake their hands if they offer one first, and you should never initiate conversation with the king or queen unless he or she addresses you first."

Oh great. How am I supposed to ask the queen about that exiting-a-limousine trick now?

Elise continues. "You will likely not have much occasion to interact with His and Her Majesty, so I shall skip ahead to the children. When introducing them, it is Her Royal Highness the Princess of Somerstein and His Royal Highness the Prince of Somerstein. To address them directly, it is Your Royal Highness. Are you able to follow?"

Dad and I both nod. What was I just saying about being all relaxed and thinking they were like me?

At Your Service

"You need only address them this way in your first exchange. Thereafter, please feel free to use 'sir' or 'madam' or Prince Alex, Princess Sophie, et cetera."

Wait, so I'm supposed to call a nine-year-old "madam"? Weird. I guess getting "the Royal Treatment" is a real, actual thing. And something I better get used to giving pretty fast, because just then three kids appear in the pool area dressed only in bathing suits and fluffy robes. Immediately two bodyguards take up a post outside the doors. Looks like the pool just became a private party.

Without a glance in our direction, Alex (*make that* Prince Alex, Prince Alex, don't forget the "Prince," Chloe) tosses his stuff over a lounge chair and does a sideways, legs-together fall into the deep end. Ingrid follows with a cannonball. Sophie carefully removes her robe and folds it neatly before placing it dead center in the middle of the chaise. She drapes a towel over the back of the chair and lines up her flip-flops underneath it. Only then does she move—or really she sashays—to the steps and enters the pool one dainty toe at a time.

A shrill whistle cuts the air. I whip my head around in time to see Elise remove two fingers from her mouth. Ingrid and Sophie exit the pool immediately and line up at attention. It's kind of creepy, like something out of *The Sound of Music*.

Alex does the backstroke over to the pool edge closest to us, flips right-side up, and hooks his elbows over the edge.

His hair is slicked back by the water. I know he's a boy in a bathing suit, so it makes total sense that he wouldn't have a shirt on, but it makes me kind of squirmy.

"Hello, Lisey," he says.

With a way cute accent. He and Elise sound mostly British, but with a hint of something else I can't place.

Elise places both hands on her hips and stares him down until he swings his leg over the edge and uses his arms to hoist himself out. He shakes the water out of his hair like he's starring in a music video. Warning bells go off in my head. Uh-oh. Egotistical much?

Still, the grin he gives Elise makes my belly do this weird flipping thing, like it's trying out a cannonball too.

Elise pushes her glasses up the bridge of her nose.

"Children, you can get right back to your swim, but first I'd like you to meet Mr. and Miss Turner. They've put together a very thoughtful and educational itinerary for your visit."

Dad bows his head. "A pleasure to meet you, Your Royal Highnesses. And actually the itinerary is all my daughter Chloe's doing. She's looking forward to showing off her hometown."

At Your Service

Sophie inclines her head down slightly in acknowledgment, like she's the pope and Dad just asked to kiss her ring or something. Sheesh. Ingrid does a funny curtsy kind of thing that makes Alex tussle her hair. He smirks at me, and it seems like he's waiting for me to say something. Anything.

What I try to say is, "Pleased to meet you, Your Highness." What I actually say is something more along the lines of, "Whfflsflshthakzc."

Ingrid giggles. Sophie places a hand delicately over her mouth to hide her smile. Alex isn't so polite.

"Gesundheit," he says with that cocky grin.

My face turns the color of the heat lamp in the sauna. Great. Just great. Apparently I'm an epic fail at meeting royals of any kind. I might as well just look for a concierge job at a roadside motel.

Elise steps in and rescues me, while Dad squeezes my shoulder. "You three may go back to your swim," she says.

Alex gives a little salute and drops back into the water. Sophie nods politely and heads for her chair instead, where she stretches out with a book. Probably *Miss Manners' Book of Perfect Etiquette for All Occasions.*

Ingrid stays in place. "Do you have any Susan B. Anthony dollars?"

Huh? Dad has moved aside and is deep in conversation with Elise, so I guess Ingrid's talking to me. Okay, well this is a good thing. Of all the royals, she's the one I'm least likely to further humiliate myself with.

"Um, I don't think so. Do you like her or something?" I ask.

"No, silly. I collect coins. I try to get one of everything from every country we visit. I even have santimats from Morocco and baht from Thailand."

"Oh, that's really cool. I can see about getting you a Susan B. Anthony dollar. Hey, if you like money, you know where we should go? The Federal Reserve on Wall Street. It's like a real-life Gringotts*. Did you read any of the Harry Potter books?"

Ingrid nods her head enthusiastically. She's really cute. I glance at Dad and Elise, hoping Dad is noticing how well I'm handling myself now, but they're both bent over some pages spread out on one of the tables. Bummer.

"The one on Wall Street probably isn't guarded by dragons, though," I say, but when I check to see how my joke went over with Ingrid, she's not there. Like totally gone, as

---

* Most people don't know that the Federal Reserve has these vaults eighty feet below the bank that hold twenty-five percent of all the gold bars in the whole world. How cool is that? Dad had a guest once who worked there. I doubt he got to ride in carts with goblins, though.

if she'd never been there to begin with. Weird. I jump up to make sure she isn't at the bottom of the pool. Nope. Only Alex swimming laps. But still, where is she? Um, should we be worried here?

"Uh, Elise?" I call. "I don't see Ingrid."

She doesn't even glance up. "Don't worry. Ingrid's like a little Houdini with her disappearing acts. She's here somewhere. The bodyguards would let us know if she reached the door."

Sure enough, when I glance back toward Sophie, there's Ingrid sitting in the chair next to her, like she'd been there the whole time. Had she? Great. Just what I need—the Incredible Invisible Girl.

She better not try to pull any disappearing acts on my watch.

Chapter Twelve

*T*he tramway dangles us in an enclosed glass box halfway across the East River. The Queensboro Bridge is so close beside us, it feels like I could reach out my window and touch it. Ingrid presses her face against the glass and makes an *oh* sound.

"Look how far down the water is," she says with a happy squeal.

"I know, pretty cool, huh?" I look to Sophie for confirmation, but she just shrugs and says, "It's basically the same thing as the ski lifts in the Alps. Only this one doesn't take us to the top of a beautiful mountain. It just takes us . . . there." Sophie points to the dingy apartment buildings and the run-down-looking pathways that line either side of the tramway station on Roosevelt Island. "What do you have planned for us when we arrive anyway?"

I swallow. "Well, nothing really. I mean, I thought we'd just turn around and go back. There's not much on Roosevelt Island. There's an ice cream shop on Main Street, but, uh, I have us down to go to Serendipity Three when we leave here and that's got great desserts, so . . ."

"So we're not going somewhere right now?"

"Well, um, it's more of a 'the journey is the destination' kind of thing. Because it's kind of neat to ride the tramway, and it has the best views of the skyline and, oh, it was in the Spider-Man movie. That's pretty cool, right, Your Highness?"

Sophie just smiles tightly. Totally fake. Alex is the one who answers. Of course, first he has to flip his hair for the hundredth time. "Ah yes. That scene where he has to rescue Mary Jane from the bridge. I thought this looked rather familiar."

At least he recognizes it, but his tone doesn't sound overly enthusiastic. Crud. So far, nothing I've come up with has seemed to make anyone other than Ingrid happy, and I have the feeling I could plop her in front of a *Welcome to New York* video at the visitors' center and she'd be plenty content.

I know I'm doing this for work and all, but I usually have

so much fun sharing my city with our guests, and I thought it would be the same with the royals. Except Alex and Sophie definitely have a "been there, done that, bought the souvenir T-shirt" attitude about anything I try to show them. I guess you get jaded pretty quickly when your summer vacations include camel treks into the Sahara and scuba diving along the Great Barrier Reef.

"Um, here, why don't you guys squeeze together so I can get your picture?" I say.

I like to give my guests a little printed photo book when they check out, so they can remember all the fun they had in Manhattan. It's part of the patented Concierge Chloe package. While Ingrid's smile is genuine, Sophie's is plastic, and Alex's is all "I'm cute and I know it."

At least I'm the only one snapping photos. None of the newspaper photographers who showed up to cover the initial arrival have made an appearance today, which I'm guessing means they're more interested in the king and queen than their kids.

So I don't get it. Except for Ingrid, why on earth do they look so bored?

At least Paisley is meeting us at Serendipity, and she gets along with everyone on earth, so maybe she can help break the ice. We make the round-trip and get off the tram on the East Side, where the two matching bodyguards hop off first to clear a path through the nonexistent crowd. Oh, and when I say matching, I really do mean matching. Hans and Frans are identical twins and, in their coordinating black suits, you really couldn't pay me to tell you who is who. One of them (Frans?) crashes down the stairs and keeps anyone from ascending to the tramway platform while we file down the metal steps. Hans brings up the rear. He keeps looking around like ninja assassins are going to come swinging down from the rafters at any second. Guess no one told him New York actually has a super-low crime rate.*

Bill has the limo door open for us by the time we reach street level.

I'm still getting a little tongue-tied when I try to talk directly to Alex, so I look at Sophie as I say, "Your Majesties, if you'd like to ride, please feel free, though we're only going about half a block up Sixtieth."

Ingrid grabs on to my hand and squeezes. Ha! At least someone likes me.

"We'll walk," says Sophie. Then she takes off at a glide

---

* It's true. Really. Google it.

ahead of me. Alex saunters along behind her like he owns the street (of course, back home, I think maybe he actually *does* own the roadways). I yank Ingrid along as we catch up and overtake them. I'm certain my weird speed walk looks nothing like Sophie's graceful swishing, but I'm too annoyed to care. Hans and Frans trail us at a respectful distance.

Ugh. This could be a long day.

Chapter Thirteen

When we reach Serendipity, Paisley is leaning against the iron-scroll fence next to the entrance. I'm super thrilled to see her, although, whereas I am dressed in another black business suit and short, patent-leather heels, Pay has on a pink Yankees hoodie, jeans, and canvas sneakers. Ergh. Does she not realize this is *royalty* we're spending the day with?

I motion Sophie and Ingrid to stop in front of Pay and wait for Alex to finish his casual stroll. Seriously. It's like he has a MAKE WAY FOR A PRINCE sign on his chest. I half expect the elephant parade Prince Ali Ababwa had to announce his arrival in *Aladdin*. Pay, to her credit, does not actually drool, though a helicopter could land in her open mouth. I step on her foot with my heel.

"Ow!" she yelps, and grabs her toes, hopping a little.

Ignoring her, I say, "Paisley, may I present His Royal Highness the Prince and Her Royal Highnesses the Princesses of Somerstein."

Pay places her foot back on the ground and sticks out a hand. "Hey. I'm Paisley."

I want to slap her forehead. *Hey? Really, Pay? Hey?*

"Hello there. I'm Alex." Alex pumps Pay's arm. "That's Sophie and Ingrid." Both wave and smile genuine smiles.

Huh.

Well, whatever.

"There's a gazillion-year wait, like there is every Saturday," Paisley says next.

"Not for us, there isn't," I reply. I slide past the clusters of tourists jamming into the tiny front part of the restaurant, where they sell souvenirs and little gift-type stuff. In less than three minutes' time, the manager is setting up a prime table underneath the giant red Pegasus that hangs on the wall. I even take the liberty of ordering us each one of their signature frozen hot chocolates. Mission accomplished. I toss my suit jacket over a chair, then return to the sidewalk.

"All set."

At Your Service

For once, Alex looks awkward. "Oh, not necessary. We can certainly wait our turn like everyone else."

I raise both eyebrows. "But our table is ready. It's no problem."

Alex kicks at a stick on the sidewalk. "No, really. We don't require any special treatment."

I just stare at him. What's the deal? I thought he'd be impressed at how competent I am at my job and how well I'm taking care of him and his sisters. But he just puts both hands in the pockets of his khakis and rocks back on his heels. The self-satisfied smile creeps back as he examines me.

This time my stomach only feels like it has a stray jumping bean or two in it, instead of a bunch of kangaroos hopping around. It's amazing how someone can get less cute the more you get to know his personality. Granted, we're still pretty far from talking "ugly," but if he keeps it up with the arrogant grins . . .

I wipe all traces of sarcasm from my voice to say, "Well, I beg your pardon, Your Majesty, but the staff has cleared space for us and, besides, if we don't eat now, we won't have time for everything on the itinerary."

Alex doesn't say anything; he just ducks through the

doorway. Our group pushes past the waiting crowd and settles into our seats.

Once we're sitting down with our frozen hot chocolates in front of us, Sophie spreads her napkin delicately across her lap. I can't imagine why she's bothering. It's not like *she* could possibly ever spill anything.

Immediately Pay begins harassing the three kids with all kinds of questions about their castle back home.

"Really, Pay, I don't think they want to talk about that," I say. As much as I wanted her here—and even Dad thought adding another kid to the mix could make it more fun for the royals—I'm starting to wonder if inviting her was the best idea. She's not exactly treating them like the royalty they are.

"Why ever not?" asks Alex, leaning back in his seat and sticking his long legs off to the side. "Quid pro quo, *Pay*."

"Quid pro what?" asks Paisley.

"Do you not have to take Latin in school, then? Shame that. It means I shall tell you something if you tell me something back."

"Oh, cool," she says. "Okay, first question. What does your bedroom look like?"

My jaw drops. Alex purses his lips together to keep from laughing, and Pay punches him on the leg for it.

At Your Service

Actually punches the Crown Prince of Somerstein.

I am *so* dead.

"I want to know if you have posters on the walls and dirty clothes all over the floor or if you have one of those, like, canopy-bed things that close off with velvet curtains."

I can't *believe* she's talking about dirty clothes to ROY-ALTY, but Alex just laughs. "You watch far too many movies. I do not have anything on the floor, but only because I have a personal valet who picks up my socks wherever I drop them. It's a bang-up perk."

I think of the housekeeping staff at the St. Michèle. Yeah, I have to agree with him there.

"And I have framed football jerseys on my wall. Or soccer, as you insist upon calling it here," Alex says.

"Cool. Any from Manchester United?" asks Pay.

Alex leans forward and rests his elbows on the table right next to her. "*You* know Man U?"

Okay, so I mean, I'm definitely not jealous because:

    A. Even though he has surfer hair and navy-like-a-night-sky eyes and an accent that could melt butter, he's also totally arrogant and annoying, so it's not like I'm even interested.

B. If I *were* interested, I would still not be
   interested, because ruining my reputation
   as the city's top (okay, well, maybe only—but
   I *would* be top if I had actual competition)
   junior concierge over a guy who seems totally
   conceited would never be worth it. Even if he is
   a prince.

C. I really need to find a C one of these days.

I decide to distract myself with someone other than the Prince of Ego, but when I look around, my frozen hot chocolate turns to paste in my mouth.

"Hey, where's Princess Ingrid?"

Chapter Fourteen

Alex and Sophie barely look up from their chocolaty goodness, and even Pay blinks a few times, as if she forgot she was sitting at a wrought-iron table in Midtown. Frans and Hans point in unison under the table. Oh. Phew. When I duck my head under, I find Ingrid there, cross-legged and taking items out of her backpack.

"What're you doing under here?" I ask in my sweetest "I'm not at all annoyed" voice.

"Was rather bored."

I kind of love the way they all speak so formally. I'll bet they have an actual governess to tutor them. Ingrid has a few Barbies spread out on top of a slew of leaflets advertising

Wicked on Broadway and double-decker-bus tours, along with maps of the city and subway. I recognize them all from the brochure case in the lobby of the St. Michèle. She's using them to form a runway for the dolls.

"That's quite a setup you have going. Hey, can I take a picture of it since we'll have to pack up soon?"

Ingrid smiles and holds a Barbie in each fist.

"Move them down a little. I can't see your pretty face." I snap a photo. She just smiles and resumes her *Project Runway* reenactment. When the rest of us finish our midmorning snack, I help Ingrid pile everything into her backpack. She's a funny girl, but I really like her.

Which is why I say, "Princess Ingrid, would you like to pick what we do next? We have options. We can walk another half block to Dylan's Candy Bar, which is the biggest candy store you've ever seen, or we can walk or drive about five blocks to FAO Schwarz, which is the biggest toy store you've ever seen. Or there's Central Park right there too."

We're making our way outside as Sophie answers for her.

"Oh, Central Park, most definitely. It will be nice to see some green amidst all this gray." She wrinkles her nose delicately.

"Gray's nothing. Just be glad it's not the 1800s because,

At Your Service

before there were garbage trucks, the city used actual pigs to keep the streets clean. They'd just snuff along and gobble up all the trash." Pay looks very proud of her New York trivia.

I choose to ignore it and produce a stat more likely to impress the ice queen, er, ice *princess*, in this case.

"Actually, Central Park has a TON of green space. It's even bigger than the entire municipality of Monaco," I say.

Try that one on for size, Princess Sophie.

But all she says is, "Oh, Monaco is so very lovely this time of year. The gardens around Uncle Philip's castle are just enchanting. Ohmygosh, Alex! We forgot his birthday!"

"Speak for yourself. I played Operation X with him for four hours before his birthday gala."

"You did? How?"

"Remote gaming headsets." Alex shrugs.

Oh sure. Because of course, remote gaming headsets are exactly what you would use to play a special-ops video game with King Philip of Monaco, while dukes and duchesses and earls wait downstairs in the ballroom in their tuxes and gowns. I mean, it's so obvious.

Who *are* these people?

"Well, I did say our next stop is Princess Ingrid's choice." I try to be diplomatic, but I'm beginning to have a hard time keeping my cool. So sorry if my hometown is imperfectly real and yours sounds like some kind of Emerald City. Where's the fun in that? New York wouldn't be New York without some grime and obnoxious taxi drivers and open delivery hatches in the sidewalk that could drop you to a bloody death. Or at least a broken fibula. That's all part of what makes it the best city anywhere, and Sophie is so busy looking down her nose, she's missing it.

Ingrid tugs on my suit leg. "If we go to FAO Schwarz, can we still go back to the candy place later?"

I smile at her. "Sure!"

Bill is waiting with the limo, so we decide to skip the walk and grab a ride. A few minutes later he deposits us in front of the real-live "toy" soldiers keeping guard over the greatest toy store on earth. I hold the door so everyone can file in. Immediately we're greeted with the song we'll all be singing for the rest of the day/week/month whether we want to or not. "Welcome to our world, welcome to our world, welcome to our world of toys . . ."

Alex groans. "Mind if I head to the Apple Store just outside instead?"

"Yes!" The rest of us answer as one. I'm surprised everyone agrees with me for once. I don't know what their motives are, but mine are clear: keep this outing as streamlined as possible. If we start splitting up now, it all turns to chaos. I grab Ingrid's hand again.

"C'mon. Upstairs there's a whole area dedicated just to Barbie."

She bounces up and down and lets me lead the way to the escalator. The others trudge behind. Hans and Frans make themselves busy peering into the cluster of life-sized stuffed Pat the Bunnies as if secret government agents could be hiding among the mountain of soft fur.

"Can I at least duck into the gentlemen's room on my own, or does that need to be a group effort too?" asks Alex when we reach the second floor.

I blush and duck my head to hide it. "We'll wait for you. It's right over there, behind the Dippin' Dots stand."

Even though we just had frozen hot chocolate, which is basically ice cream, Paisley and Sophie wander over to check out the flavors. Ingrid spies something just beyond.

"What's that?" She points at a souvenir penny press.

"C'mon, I'll show you. You're a coin collector; I'll bet you like this. You pick out the design you want, then stick a penny in this part here and two quarters here. Crank the handle around until it gets really hard to turn. And then a penny pops out. But it's all flattened and it has the design you picked out on it. See, you can choose from a teddy bear, a toy soldier, a princess, or a train. And they all say 'FAO Schwarz' on them so you can remember where you got it."

Ingrid has her face pushed up against the machine like it's whispering the secret of life to her. She's still standing like this a full minute later when Alex exits the men's room and comes over to join us.

"What's this?"

"It's a penny machine. You really don't have these in Europe?"

"Well, considering we don't have *pennies* in Europe . . ."

Oh. Right.

Ingrid tugs at Alex's shirt. "Please, please can we get them?"

I take charge. "Sure! Let me see if I have some change in my wallet. And I'll bet downstairs they sell little folding books that are designed to hold collections of these."

Alex rumples Ingrid's hair and smiles. "Just what this monkey needs—another coin collection."

"I do! I really do! Chloe, are there more of these?"

I shrug. "Sure, they're all over the city. We can look up where there are others."

I hand over a fistful of change to Ingrid, and she busies

herself making one of each design. She doesn't even want to see the Barbie section after that. All she can focus on is going downstairs to buy the collector's book to store her new treasures in. When she spots a second penny machine on the first floor, she goes crazy. Um, yeah. I thought I cared about my collection of hotel postcards, but this girl seriously loves her coins.

We can't find any of the collector books, but I stand in line to change a ten-dollar bill into a roll of quarters and swap one quarter for twenty-five pennies. This should last us their visit.

At least one person is on her way to happy.

Chapter Fifteen

When we leave FAO Schwarz, Ingrid is a girl on a mission, but I manage to convince her that everyone gets a vote on where we go next. Alex is still yammering on about the Apple Store, and Sophie spots all the horse-drawn carriages lined up across the street at the entrance to Central Park. I would have thought she caught a ride to school every day in one of those, but I guess not, because she's doing some serious fangirling.

"Princess Ingrid, how about we let these guys head in to Apple, and we'll grab you a pink lemonade at the FAO Café before we meet back up with them. Sound good?"

The not-splitting-up thing? Totally only applies when it isn't my idea.

At Your Service

Pay pulls me aside as everyone else chats on the sidewalk. "How're ya holding up? You seem kind of . . . tense."

I give her a smile to let her know how glad I am that she's here after all, even if she does insist on being overly casual with actual royalty.

"I'm just trying to follow all the protocols and make sure everybody's happy every second of the day. Speaking of which, I heard you call Alex 'Alex,' but remember what I told you yesterday? Elise says we have to call them Prince and Princess before their names."

"Yeah, but he introduced himself to me as Alex, not Prince Alex."

I puff my hair out of my face. I don't have time to argue the point with Pay, and as long as *I* continue to follow instructions, I think I'm okay. "It's kind of a lot of pressure," I say. "I mean, I'm used to that from other guests, but I guess I'm also used to guests who are a little more into the whole tourist thing."

"I hear ya. On the other hand, these guys probably see their share of foreign cities and have to deal with different handlers everywhere they go. Not that you're just a 'handler'! I only mean they probably get tired of having new people sucking up to them all the time and . . . yeah, none of this is coming out right."

Jen Malone

I snort and she laughs.

"Just try to relax and have fun. That's what I really wanted to say." Pay shrugs her shoulders.

"Easy for you to say. You don't have to be 'the very embodiment of the Saint Michèle brand.'" I roll my eyes as I recite Dad's words. He's right, though; that *is* a concierge's job and I get it.

Pay studies me for a second. "Maybe these guys would have a better time spending the day with Chloe versus a hotel brand. I'm just saying . . ."

Again, easy for her. I can't do anything the least bit out of line that would get back to Dad or Elise or—I shudder just thinking about it—the king and queen. If that means I have to take my job seriously while everyone else has fun, well, that's kind of what I signed on for.

Pay gives me a quick hug and goes to join up with the others. Frans (or Hans maybe?) stays behind with Ingrid and me, while the other three and Hans (or possibly Frans) go off to play with toys that are more their speed. I order Ingrid her lemonade and then steer us to meet up with the group.

The Apple Store on Fifth Avenue is way cool. It's basically this giant glass box that, on cloudy days, shows the reflection of the Plaza Hotel across the street (hi, Eloise!). And then you have to walk down all these stairs to get to the actual store part underground. I have no idea how they even built it. And the best part is it never closes, so if you really, really have to get an iPod Touch at three o'clock in the morning, they've got you covered.

Inside there's this wide spiral staircase made out of phobia stairs. That's what I call stairs that don't have a back part to them, just the part you step on. I know I'm not actually small enough to slip through the gap between them, because it's probably less than a foot tall or something, but I really, really, REALLY hate going up or down stairs like that. Going up is worse because I can see the gaps more clearly, but I still get nervous going down.

Which doesn't work out so well in this case. I'm going extra slow, and Ingrid doesn't seem to do anything extra slow, so she's literally stepping on my heels as I go down each stair. That makes me even more irrationally nervous that I'm going to slip right through the back of the stairs and split my skull open on the really expensive-looking marble floor. So I come to a complete stop.

Unfortunately Ingrid doesn't.

She goes tumbling. Not through the slats, because I KNOW, that isn't even logical, but just down two steps and right into Frans's or Hans's back. Luckily, it's like crashing into a steel wall because he's all bodyguard muscular, so she stops right away. Not so luckily, she had her full cup of pink lemonade in her hands, so now Frans/Hans is wearing it. He doesn't look too excited about this. A small river of pink liquid *does* slide through the gap in the steps and onto the floor below.

"Are you okay?" I push my phobia aside and race down the steps to where Ingrid is rubbing her arm. Returning a guest in a full body cast is probably not going to look good on my Les Clefs d'Or application.

"I think Frans might be a Transformer. He hurts to run into," Ingrid says. At least she can joke. That has to be a good sign. I grab her arm and help her up. And (bonus!) now I know which bodyguard is dripping pink sugar all over the spiral staircase.

"Sorry, Frans," mumbles Ingrid.

"At least you are safe," he answers, but I can see him trying not to wince when he sticks his leg out and his pants cling to him like a wetsuit.

"We can hang here if you want Bill to take you back to the Saint Michèle for a different suit. It's super close by," I tell him.

Frans looks like he's debating the safety protocol involved, but one step and a sloshing shoe is all it takes for him to see the light. He calls his brother, and they have a lightning-speed conversation in some foreign language.

"I will go with your driver and be right back. You all stay here with Hans," Frans says.

"Okeydokey."

Frans starts up the staircase and Ingrid and I head down. I'm totally taking the elevator when it's time to go.

We catch up with Alex, Sophie, and Pay by the iPads. It looks like they've found some way to play a game against each other on the demo devices, and they're tilting the tablets from side to side in their hands. Pay picks up her head to smile hi, but the other two barely acknowledge us.

Lovely.

Ingrid tugs at my suit-jacket sleeve. "You said we could find more penny machines."

"I don't think there are any in here, Princess."

Her shoulders slump. Is she going to cry? Oh no. No, no, no. I have a strict rule against any of my guests crying while in my care.

"Hey, I have an idea. Why don't we use one of these computers to look for a list of other penny machines in the city?"

I find a vacant iMac and Google "penny presses New York City." Sure enough, within seconds I have a list of about twenty machines.

"Hey, there are some cool places on here. The Bronx Zoo, Coney Island, New York Aquarium . . . Times Square. We can definitely hit up some of these."

Ingrid crosses her arms. "All of them."

"All of them? Oh no, I don't think we have time for that this trip. The Bronx Zoo alone looks like it has eight separate machines. That's a whole afternoon right there. And Coney Island would take us way over an hour to get to. We can go to the ones in Times Square and, hey, there's one at the Central Park Zoo. That one's only about a five-minute walk from here. Don't worry, we'll get you a great collection."

Ingrid stares at me, and suddenly her freckles look a little less cute and a little more menacing.

"All of them."

"Princess Ingrid, er, madam, it can't be done. The one in Yankee Stadium is inside the gates. That means you can only get in there when a game is going on."

"Is there a game today?" Now her foot is tapping.

"The team's still in Florida for spring training. I think they have tours of the stadium, but we'd have to really rush to get there in time. They only have them around lunchtime unless you arrange it ahead of time. But I'll tell you what, you go stand with your brother and sister, and I'll see if I can talk someone here into getting me a printout of these spots, okay? We can circle the ones we can get to."

The girl I ask is really friendly, but insists that the Apple Store isn't a copy center. I have to use my best concierge charm (it helps when I produce a business card; it isn't exactly hotel-issued, but you can get anything off the Internet these days). I finally manage to score a hard copy of the penny machine locations, which I tuck into my wallet.

When Ingrid spots me coming, she pushes between Sophie and Alex and puts one hand over each of their iPads. They both yelp.

"Ingrid! I was winning," Alex shouts.

"You most definitely were not, Prince of Suck It," replies Pay with a smirk. Prince of Suck It? She just called him Prince of Suck It. I almost wish I'd crashed through the phobia steps after all. But Alex grins back.

Ingrid seems unconcerned. "We're leaving," she announces.

"We are not," says Alex. Sophie begins pulling at her lip with her thumb. It's obvious she wants nothing to do with any kind of conflict. Maybe that's how she stays so regal all the time. Just avoid all unpleasantness and live happily ever after in Dreamland. Wish I was there now.

Instead I have to solve this problem, like the good concierge I am. "Look, Princess Ingrid is on a mission of sorts. She wants to collect more pennies. Since Princess Sophie said she wants to see Central Park next, maybe we could head to the zoo there. It's not far from here, and then everyone will have gotten a chance to do something they wanted." I exhale and hope this plan works for everyone. It sounds perfectly logical to me.

Too bad the three faces staring back at me don't seem to agree. You know that saying, "You can't please all the people all the time"? Right now I'm not pleasing any of the people any of the time. Sophie wants to see Central Park, but only in a carriage. Ingrid wants to zoom in and out of Central Park as fast as possible so we can head to the next spot on her penny-press list. And Alex? Who knows what he wants. I guess to finish his game.

Luckily, Pay is the bestest of best friends. "I'm with Chloe. It's stuffy down here. Let's check out the park."

Alex scowls. "I really need to ask someone at the Genius Bar about a problem I'm having with my phone first. It's not connecting my international calls. Can we at least do that while we're here?"

At Your Service

Sophie and Pay nod. I don't see why he couldn't have handled that BEFORE playing a game, but I nod too. Ingrid is wearing a small storm cloud over her head and she doesn't say anything. We give Alex's name at the Genius Bar and, while we wait his turn, Sophie challenges Pay to another round of the game they'd all been playing. I watch over her shoulder and it actually looks like a fun one.

When we finish, I do a quick head count. Frans (wait, it's Hans, right? Oh drat, now I can't remember anymore) is over by Alex, who's talking to the Apple genius. (FYI: If I couldn't be a concierge, I'd want to work somewhere where my actual job title is "genius.") Sophie is wandering over to look at the cell phone cases. Pay is right next to me and Ingrid is—

WHERE IS INGRID?

Chapter Sixteen

The whole place is one big box with a staircase in the middle, so it isn't like there's anywhere to hide. I scan the entire room, while my stomach feels like the Empire State Building dropped into it.

"Princess Ingrid?" I yell, and Sophie's head jerks up. Alex and Frans/Hans don't seem to hear, but Pay clues in right away. Sophie materializes at my elbow within a thump or two of my hammering heart. My whole insides are basically a construction zone.

"Shh!!!" she says.

"Why shh? I can't find your sister!"

"I know, but I don't want to get her in trouble with Hans." So it's Hans. Hans, Hans, Hans. I try to imprint that on my memory before I realize I don't actually give a fig which one he is. I LOST MY GUEST!

Sophie grabs my hand. I'm momentarily surprised her skin feels like real-person skin and not like a marble statue or something.

"She's always up to nonsense like this and Dad says if she disappears again, she can't have a pony for her birthday."

For real?

I just—

I don't even know what to say to a statement like that.

Sophie whispers, "Well, there's also that Dad's been mentioning military school for Alex, and if he learns we let Ingrid out of our sight . . ."

I sneak a glance at Alex. He's pointing to something on his phone, happily oblivious to our megacrisis.

Sophie follows my look and says, "I'll get him. He'll know what to do. You two just look around under the tables or something. But don't be *obvious*."

Don't be obvious crawling around on the floor of the Apple Store? Luckily, this is New York, and the Apple Store is crazy crowded.

Pay and I split up and do a quick sweep of the store. One of my eyes remains on Hans, and whenever he glances around,

I quickly pretend to be examining whichever techie device is closest. Sophie says something to Alex, and he leaves Hans talking to Mr. Genius guy while he saunters over to me like he doesn't have a care in the world. Paisley and Sophie join us.

"She's not anywhere?" His body is all casual floppy, but his voice has a decidedly uncool edge to it. Good. At least someone is freaking out with me.

I shake my head. I'm not sure I trust my voice to come out anything other than pip-squeaky.

Sophie takes charge. "Okay. Be Ingrid. Let's put ourselves in her shoes. Where would she go?"

Thunk. My stomach slides all the way into my patent-leather heels. I reach into my purse, already sure of what I'll find there. Which is nothing.

"She took it."

"Took what?" Alex asks.

"My wallet. It had the list of penny machine locations. And the quarters, all my cash, plus my MetroCard. Everything she'd need. Omigosh. She's going to try to get to all the machines."

"So she's alone . . . up there?" Pay's chin jerks toward heaven, but I know she really means street level. And not "up there" but "out there."

At Your Service

As in 100 percent all alone in New York City.

"We gotta go after her! I'm positive she'd go to the Central Park Zoo first. I told her how close we were to it. If we run, we can catch her," I say, trying to keep the panic out of my voice. I don't think I do a very good job.

"We have to lose Hans first." Alex is matter-of-fact.

"Are we allowed to do that?" I gape at him. This may be an emergency, but I still have protocol on my mind.

"Quite right we're not. But if he's along, he'll tell Father right away and our gooses will be cooked."

I suddenly have an even worse thought.

If Alex's dad finds out, that means my dad finds out. I can kiss my Capable Chloe nickname good-bye, right alongside my golden key from Les Clefs d'Or. I'll have to be an architect or a scientist or something totally boring instead of the greatest concierge in the history of New York City. This is now officially a megadisaster!

Okay, so maybe Hans would be the one in actual trouble, because technically, he should have been watching Ingrid, but just because he didn't do his job doesn't mean I shouldn't do mine. My job is to help my guests get what they want, and what they want is to ditch Hans. So, um, aren't I kind of obligated to do as they wish? My throat has a knot in it like it's trying to tell me this isn't the best idea, but I swallow it away.

"Let's ditch Hans," I say. "Except won't he call in the police to find all of us, then?"

"Doubtful. He'll chalk it up to a prank and figure we're safe, especially since he knows you know the city so well. We're always trying to get a little freedom from our bodyguards, so he won't think anything's actually wrong. Besides, five of us on our own is totally different than one nine-year-old alone in the city. He probably won't want to get in trouble for letting us give him the slip, so odds are fifty-fifty he even tells Father. My guess is he and Frans will try to find us themselves."

Alex heads back over to the Genius Bar, and I see him yukking it up with Hans and the Apple guy. How can he even fake laugh at a time like this? Then he leads Hans off in the direction of the restroom. While Hans is distracted, Alex places his hand down by his leg and makes a little pushing motion, telling us to move it. We're halfway up the phobia steps (and the fact that I don't even pause to contemplate them is a definite first) when Alex comes tearing around the corner from the bathroom.

"Go!" he yells.

Slamming out the glass doors, we book it for the entrance to Central Park. I barely pay attention to the traffic we dodge between. I do notice when Alex maneuvers to the outside of

Pay, Sophie, and me, so that he'd get flattened by the crush of yellow taxis before we would. He might be sort of full of himself, but if that isn't true princely behavior, I don't know what is.

We thud down the pathway into the park, flying by people enjoying the early spring day on the green benches. We barrel past the hot dog carts and the soft pretzel carts and the ice cream carts. We zoom past the street artists sketching carica-tures and weave around rollerbladers, until we stop, huffing and puffing, in front of the zoo entrance.

I usually love walking the pathway alongside the zoo, especially when it's time for the musical clock to chime and the brass animals to march along the top of the brick archway. Obviously, I am not noticing the clock now. I give only a sliver of attention to the seal enclosure, even though there's a crowd gathering, which means it must be close to feeding time. I spin in place at the zoo entrance: the café . . . the restrooms . . . the ticket booth . . . THERE! The penny machines (there are two of them) sit tucked to the edge of the brick walkway, right by the gift shop. These are more modern looking than the ones at FAO, but one thing is decidedly missing: Ingrid. There are chil-dren everywhere, but not one single ponytailed, freckled-faced Somersteinian. Somersteiner? Somersteiny?

Doesn't matter. She's not here.

We all spread out in different directions. I choose the pathway under the musical clock that links the main zoo with the Children's Zoo. I'm so frantic, I can't even remember what Ingrid is wearing, so I peer into the face of every girl I pass. There are blondes, brunettes, redheads, girls in hats, girls in hoodies, girls on their dads' shoulders. There are no princesses. Or at the very least, there is no Princess Ingrid.

I turn and do the same systematic check back to the penny machines, where everyone else is already waiting. I hold my breath in the crazy hope that Ingrid will pop out from behind Alex's legs and we'll all hug, and by later this afternoon we'll be laughing and joking about the scare she gave us. But all I have to do is look at Sophie's face to know that isn't going to happen.

Sophie takes her royal role waaaay too seriously, but I will give the girl this: So far, she's looked like she was ready to hold court with her subjects at a moment's notice. Not now. Her eyes are all wild, like Mr. Whilpers when he realizes I bought up every last one of his precious Dr Peppers from the break-room soda machine.

We are so dead.

Chapter Seventeen

What do we do now?" Sophie shrieks, and grabs Alex's arm. He puts it around her and strokes her hair gently.

I feel like I should be the one to take charge here. Here's the thing: If you want to pay homage to the *Breakfast at Tiffany's* movie by actually having breakfast on the sidewalk outside Tiffany's, I can secure a café table and a delicious assortment of croissants. If you want to sit next to Spike Lee courtside at a Knicks game, I'm your girl. Organizing a search party for a missing princess who could be anywhere in the city at the moment? Um, I'm not so sure I'm qualified.

Luckily, Alex steps in. How very princely.

"Okay, let's all keep our wits about us. Whatever we do, we

can't let Father find out just yet. We're the ones who were supposed to be keeping an eye on her, and Father will have our heads if we've shirked our responsibilities. As well, I think we can find her on our own. If I'm going to be king one day, I don't want to go running to dear old Daddy every time I have a problem."

Interesting. So Alex is also trying to show his dad how capable he is? This makes me like him a teensy-tiny bit more.

Sophie doesn't seem to feel the same rush of respect. "Heavens no. I don't care if Father does follow through on his threat of military school for you, Alex. This isn't like when it happens at home."

"Um, happens at home?" Pay asks. She just beats me to it.

Sophie and Alex exchange a look before Sophie answers. "Ingrid's been sneaking off the castle grounds since she was about five. Mother and Father actually think it's good for her to learn her way in the world, so they sort of encourage it. Or at least they don't punish her."

She takes a jagged-sounding breath. "Everyone in our kingdom knows she does this and they keep an eye on her."

"Everyone in your kingdom? Everyone?" I know her country is small, but what, are they on a first-name basis with all the commoners?

"You could fit seven Somersteins inside New York City.

At Your Service

We're the fifth-smallest country in the world. There are probably more people in one city block here than there are in Saint Mert, where our castle is." Sophie's voice loses its raggedness. In fact, she sounds a little defensive. Whoops.

"Sorry, Princess Sophie." It won't do me any good to annoy my guests now. With one missing, I need to make doubly sure to keep the other two extra happy.

She smooths her not-a-strand-out-of-place hair. "My mother set up a hotline and people call in when they spot her. Then my father sends a bodyguard to trail her after the first phone call comes in. Ingrid doesn't know that. But of course, that's back home, where no one would harm her. She knows she's not allowed to behave like that here, and Mother and Father talked to her about it before we left. She swore she understood. They have all sorts of punishments lined up for her if she gets up to mischief here."

What I want to know is why didn't we hear about this ahead of time? Why weren't there ten more Hanses and Franses assigned to us? Why would Frans have left us at the Apple Store knowing Ingrid's past history of escape acts? If he were still trailing slushy footprints behind us, none of this would have happened. If I'd known, I wouldn't have taken my eyes off her, not even for a second.

But I hadn't known.

I turn to Alex, even though Sophie was the one talking. "I picked up on the fact that Ingrid liked to hide, but I didn't know she actually takes off. Why didn't you tell us so we could have kept eagle eyes on her?"

Alex looks sheepish. Good. I'm sure I've already crossed a line with the way I've just challenged him, but at the moment, I couldn't care less. Forget protocol.

"We didn't think it would be a problem," he says. "We had the bodyguards with us, and she really did seem like she understood how dangerous New York City is, so we didn't imagine . . ."

I bite my tongue. Seriously, people. One of the safest big cities in the United States. That's right. But I guess maybe not for a nine-year-old all alone. Now I'm starting to get even more worried about her because reality is settling in.

"So what do we do now? We have no idea where she's going next, or even if she came this way to begin with," Sophie asks, and now she's moved on to twisting strands of hair around her finger. I really wish Queen Caroline could have skipped the hotline and gone straight for implanting Ingrid with a homing device, like a nice, responsible parent.

Wait. Homing device.

At Your Service

Dad's been letting me watch *Law & Order* ever since I got a guest a walk-on role while they were shooting in Madison Square Park. On that show they're always triangulating cell phone signals to figure out where the bad guy is. I don't want to involve the authorities, but at this point, if it means an easy fix . . .

"Hey, does Princess Ingrid have a cell phone? Maybe we could trace the signal and figure out where she is."

Alex and Sophie just look at me. "She's only nine!" says Sophie.

Okay, so how am I supposed to know King Robert and Queen Caroline follow the pretty standard "no phone until your twelfth birthday" rule? Geez, for royalty, they sure are really . . . normal.

Alex groans. "But *we* do. If we don't want Hans and Frans on our tails in five minutes, we'd better turn ours off. I don't think they'd call in the authorities, but we've never actually all taken off like this, so I'm not totally sure what measures they'll take."

I taste something like acid in the back of my mouth. This is getting way out of hand. I probably shouldn't even be worrying about my future as a concierge. I should probably be worrying more about my future as a person. Because Dad? Is going to kill me.

Alex can tell the rest of us are on the fence. "Please, everyone! Trust me. We can do this. We just need to be smart and think like Ingrid. Turn off your phones."

Pay reaches into the front pocket of her hoodie and pulls out her flip phone. She hits the power button without a word. Then she goes right back to cranking pennies through the machine. It suddenly registers with me what she's doing.

"Pay, *what* are you doing?"

"Mostly, I'm just trying to stay out of the way while you guys figure out what you want to do. But I figure, *when* we find Ingrid, I can give her these in case she didn't actually beat us here."

When we find Ingrid. I really, really like the sound of that. But do I actually think we can do this on our own? Should I just call Dad and let him take over? I mean, I'm definitely in over my head, and I obviously don't want anything bad to happen to Ingrid. But at the same time, I know New Yorkers, and we're a lot nicer than our reputation. Half the time, even those "ripped from the headlines" cases on *Law & Order* are taken from newspaper stories in Detroit or Poughkeepsie or something. I honestly do believe she'll be safe. I just hope she isn't too scared. Can we actually figure out where she's headed next?

At Your Service

My thoughts spin around like they're on the Zenobio ride at Coney Island. For every point I come up with, my brain comes up with an "on the other hand." I just don't know. If we can find Ingrid safe and sound and get her back to the St. Michèle, everything will take care of itself.

And if we can't . . .

I don't even want to think about it.

I face Alex. "I think we should call my dad and yours." I make my decision. This is definitely the responsible thing to do.

Alex places his hands on his hips. "We're *not* going to do that."

"Princess Ingrid's all alone in the city. She doesn't know where she's going, and she's just a kid."

"Of the two of us, which of us knows Ingrid better? Which of us knows how clever she is and how well she takes care of herself?"

"Of the two of us, which one of us is in charge of today?" Now *my* hands are on *my* hips. Two can play this game.

Alex arches an eyebrow as if to suggest that I might only think I'm running this show. In a way he's right. The guest is actually always the one calling the shots. Crud. I narrow my eyes so he won't think he won that point. He is seriously so annoying. He's all obsessed with his hair and being in charge. How did I ever think he was so cute?

He barely blinks before talking again. "And of the two of us, which one of us is related to the missing person? She's *my* sister. Don't you think I'd be the one arguing hardest for whichever solution would keep her safe? Here's the thing. When you run a country, you're responsible for the people of your country even more than for your own family. We can't embarrass our father and therefore our whole country by causing a citywide search for a little girl on a penny spree. Imagine what CNN would do with that."

"So what, we just sacrifice Princess Ingrid's safety so you can save your reputation?" Some brother. But I can already see on Alex's face that he's all torn up about this. He might be annoying to argue with, but it doesn't seem like he's totally heartless.

"Of course not. If I truly thought Ingrid was in actual danger, I'd already be ringing the authorities. But I don't. I think she's on her quest and she's fine. And I think we're clever enough to scoop her up and get her back home before anyone is the wiser. Actually, I don't *think* we are; I *know* we are. You just have to trust me. Now please, we can't waste any more time. If we're going to find her, we must get searching."

At Your Service

I stare at him for a long time, my thoughts still all topsy-turvy. Paisley and Sophie are wisely staying out of things. Pay continues cranking penny designs, even though I can tell she's listening to every word, and Sophie has abandoned her hair twirls for biting her cuticles.

So it's up to me. My belly feels all hollow, like when I know I've done really badly on a history test, only this is even more serious than a grade.

Then I remember who I am and whose city this is. I am *the* best junior concierge in town and this is *my* city. We can do this. Ingrid will be fine because we'll find her in no time at all. It's barely lunchtime. We'll have her home for tea. I'm not actually sure what time tea is usually served, because the St. Michèle doesn't do high tea, but I do know it's sometime in the afternoon.

Failure is not an option. Mr. Whilpers said that the last time the AAA reviewer stayed at the hotel and we were vying for our five-diamond rating. Without a word to Alex, I pull out my phone and power it down. Sophie does the same.

He exhales. "Okay, now we need a plan."

I jump in. He might have decided what we're doing, but Capable Chloe is calling the shots on how we're doing it. "We need a hard copy of that list of penny machines. We could go back to the Apple Store and get another printed. We also need a picture of Princess Ingrid we can show people. I have a few on my phone, but if you don't want me to keep turning it on and off, we'll have to get one of those printed too."

Alex pushes his hair out of his eyes. "We can't go back to the Apple Store. Too risky. Hans could still be there searching for us or thinking we'd be coming back. And Frans could have returned too by now."

Think, Chloe, think. Where can I get access to a computer around here? I look up to the sky as if an answer will come floating down, but when I peer above the treetops, my eyes hit on the roofline of the first building I see, and I know exactly what to do.

The Plaza!

Hotels can solve any dilemma.

Or at the very least, any dilemma of the "I need something printed" variety.

"I know where to go. Follow me," I order, taking off in a half run/half walk back up the pathway.

Chapter Eighteen

The Plaza Hotel is what everyone imagines when they think of a fancy New York City hotel. Partly because of the Eloise books, and partly because it's always showing up in movies.

Of course I might be biased, but I think the St. Michèle is way, *way* better. Though I will say this, the Plaza has us beaten hands down in one category: location, location, location. The St. Michèle is only a couple blocks from Central Park on the Upper West Side, but the Plaza is right on top of it. Plus it has all this cool history—like it's an actual National Historic Landmark and the Beatles stayed there once. But who cares? We have rock stars as guests too. And kings and queens now. So there! Obviously, you'll never get me to be disloyal to my own hotel.

I come to an abrupt stop as we stand in front of the entrance. The Pulitzer Fountain is to our backs and behind that, across the street, is the Apple Store. I hope we're far enough away that Frans and Hans can't spot us if they're still there. Ahead of us are red-carpeted steps and lots of polished brass.

"Let me hide between you guys," I say.

"Pardon?" asks Sophie.

"The concierge here knows me. He'd ask a bunch of questions and probably call my dad. Hopefully, he's not even working today, but just in case, block me with your body."

Alex gives me an amused look out of the corner of his eye. My heart gives a little squeeze, and immediately I'm totally disgusted with it, because, *Hell-ooo, heart? We're annoyed with him, remember? Plus, we're supposed to be worrying about a missing girl here, not falling apart at looks from her conceited brother who thinks he's in charge.*

"Just do it, okay?" Luckily, Pay slides right into place at my side. Love that girl.

Sophie stands close on the other side of me, but not too close. Alex takes command (of course!) and steps out front. His tall body blocks mine completely. Except now I'm only an inch from his back and I can smell his boy scent. It's not a boy smell like gym socks and day-old cheese either. More like root beer and dryer sheets.

Focus, Chloe. He probably bottles that scent and rolls around in it just to have this effect on girls.

We shuffle inside. It's pretty awkward trying to walk like this. We go up the carpeted steps and through the glass revolving doors guarded by a doorman. If he thinks it's totally weird that we're moving like our legs are tied together, he doesn't comment. We enter the ornate lobby. Seriously. It looks like a museum or a villa in Rome or something, with the marbled floors and velvet-curtained windows so tall that even if all four of us stood on each other's shoulders, the person on top probably still couldn't see out the highest pane. Enormous crystal chandeliers hang from the golden ceilings. A wide staircase curls up to a second floor, but we move away from that and toward the check-in desk beside it. As Paisley's arms move front to back, I can see between the gaps. Several people in the lobby are giving us weird looks. Not good.

"Psst!" I hiss.

Alex comes to an abrupt halt and I crash into his back. He spins around and puts both arms around me to steady me. WHOA! If anything, that makes me even more off balance.

"Are you okay?" he asks. I nod. He looks into my face,

and I go all blank for a few seconds, like I've been touched in a game of freeze tag. Up close, his eyes are as blue as dark-wash jeans.

Pay tugs on my arm, and I realize we're attracting attention. Time to find my voice . . . and fast.

"Why'd you stop?" she asks.

"Oh. Um, I'm gonna hide behind that flower arrangement. We look too silly to go up to reception like, uh, like *this*." I manage to croak out the words while tearing my eyes away from Alex's. Well, hello there, frog. Hope you're enjoying hanging out in my throat.

Alex drops his arms.

Before it can get any weirder, I duck behind the table holding the arrangement and maneuver my body so that the giant vase of flowers is camouflaging as much of me as possible. You wouldn't think I'd be such a natural at this, but this enormous bouquet of fresh flowers isn't a lot bigger than the one in our lobby, and if you knew Mr. Whilpers, you too would be a master at hiding behind elaborate floral arrangements.

Safely tucked in place, I watch as Alex, Sophie, and Paisley approach a smiling woman at the check-in desk. Well, I say "check-in desk," but really it's a giant slab of marble even Alex, tall as he is, can barely see over. Sophie and Pay hover off to the side.

Right away Alex takes charge, as I expected. "Pardon me, but I need to have some documents printed. Would you possibly be able to help me procure them?"

Whoa. Boy has mad skills; he's talking her language. I'll bet he's also giving her flirty-flirty eyes and the grin where only one corner of his mouth goes up and it looks like he has a joke he wants to share with you.

Too bad this woman is a pro too. Plus, prince or not, Alex is a little young for her.

"Are you a guest of the hotel, sir?"

I push my glasses up the bridge of my nose. *Say yes, say yes.* I try to send him telepathic messages, but even though we had a definite connection a few minutes ago, I guess our brain waves aren't quite aligned.

"No, I'm not. I'm staying with my parents, the King and Queen of Somerstein, at the Hotel Saint Michèle. However, I'm in a terrible hurry and the situation is a bit desperate, so I don't have time to return there at the moment. I'd be most grateful if you could find it in your heart to help."

The thing is, most people don't actually expect to see a famous person while they're going about their regular

Jen Malone

business, but I would think this woman would give him the benefit of the doubt about who he says he is because:

A. We're in New York City. Lots of famous people live and work in New York City, and even more of them visit here.
B. We're at the Plaza Hotel. Even though it kills me to admit it, because *I* think they should all be at the St. Michèle, lots of those famous people who visit New York stay at the Plaza.
C. I think I pretty much covered it with A and B.

But Desk Clerk Girl must not be up-to-date on her subscription to the Most Eligible Royal Bachelors newsletter. It's true the British monarchy gets way more tabloid ink, but I imagine people would at least think Alex looks familiar in a "can't quite place him, but I think he's *somebody*" way. Guess not, because her face has an expression I recognize. It's the "oh why do I always have to deal with the riffraff" look I see on our front-desk clerks' faces whenever someone is insisting she didn't eat the candy bar in her room's minibar, even though the wrapper is sticking out of her pocket and the corners of her mouth are all chocolaty.

At Your Service

Offer her money. My legs are twitchy, and I have to grasp the edge of the table the flowers are resting on, because I want so badly to rush over there and resolve this. I could have those printouts in two seconds flat. I speak hotel. Actually, anyone can speak hotel. It goes like this: C-A-S-H.

All Alex has to do is slip her a twenty-dollar bill, and she'd stop looking down the tip of her nose at the three of them. The thing that's killing me is he could probably afford way more than twenty. He could even offer to name a street in Somerstein after her, probably. Or designate a holiday in her honor.

But he doesn't seem to catch on. He's probably never had to bribe anyone for anything in his entire life. What could a prince want that someone wouldn't just hand him?

"May I have your full name, sir?" Uh-oh. You don't get to work the front desk at the Plaza until you've been around the block a few times, and right about now I'm guessing Desk Clerk Girl has Alex, Sophie, and Pay pegged for a bunch of kids playing some kind of prank or something. I'll bet they get their share of that here.

Alex had been leaning in to the reception desk, but now he straightens to his full height and puffs out his chest a little bit. He looks like a rooster. A kind of cute rooster, but still.

"Since you asked, my full name is His Royal Highness, Alex Alistair Hamilton Windemere, Prince by the Grace of God, Grand Duke in Waiting of Shenkenburg, Duke Elect of Astoria, Vice-Count Palatine of the Rhine, Vice-Count of Sasr, Romitostein, Westlundair, and Chern, Burgrave in Waiting of Galenstein, Lord in Waiting of Rewerberg, Maculbaden, Bergerstein, Roslinberg, Lumburg, and Appelstein."

Pay tries to cover her giggle, but can't. "I'll bet you don't have a lot of monogrammed towels," she says, still snickering.

Alex looks at her and grins. "Can't ever find any of those personalized key chains at the souvenir shops either. Don't understand why."

But Desk Clerk Chick is not giggling. She looks ready to call security.

"You could Google me if you want," Alex offers helpfully.

She fixes him with a stern look. "That won't be necessary, Mr. Grand Du—Mr. Vice—um, sir. I'll just speak to my manager for a moment. Please wait here."

Oh, not good. I know where this is headed and it's nowhere we want to be. We're about to be politely escorted from the premises. I need to have a Plan B before I yank everyone out of here, so I try to think of where I've seen a copy shop in this part of the city. It sucks not having my iPhone turned on. It's practically become my brain substitute in the last year I've owned it.

And then I hear the one thing I've dreaded hearing since we set foot inside.

"Is that my Chloe I see?" echoes across the hushed lobby of the Plaza Hotel.

Oh. No.

Chapter Nineteen

I step out from behind the flowers and try to look like I've been admiring the arrangement instead of hanging out in surveillance mode. For good measure I sniff one of the flowers deeply, but it smells like skunk and I end up sputtering.

"Hi (cough), Ernio (cough, cough)."

The Plaza's concierge grabs me up in a giant bear hug that lifts my feet off the ground.

"I haven't seen my favorite girl since the holidays. How's my Chloe?"

We go to Ernio's every year for Thanksgiving. Some people collect ceramic animals or snow globes, but Ernio collects people. Then he invites all of them to his apartment for deep-fried turkey and pasta. It's super yummy.

"I didn't know you'd be here," I say, trying to sound all casual.

Ernio looks at me like I just did the chicken dance across the lobby. "Where else would I be?"

"Oh—well—um, I don't know, I guess."

By now Alex, Sophie, and Pay have wandered over.

"Are these your friends, Chlo?" Ernio asks.

Alex's eyebrow does that archy thing again. My stomach does that flippity-floppity thing. This could get old.

"Ernio, this is Paisley and, um, Kristoff and his sister, uh, Svetlana." I introduce them around. It's a good thing Sophie has trained her face to be pleasant in any situation, because she doesn't even register surprise that I've just assigned her a totally fake name in case Ernio follows the news more than the desk clerk. And where I got Kristoff and Svetlana, I seriously have NO IDEA.

"Nice to meet you all," Ernio says with an eyebrow wiggle of his own. Funny how my tummy doesn't even react.

"Um, actually, Ernio . . ." I pause. I don't want to give away anything about Ingrid because I don't want Ernio calling Dad. It's the same reason I gave Sophie and Alex fake names. But then again, I doubt we're going to get any help from the front-desk clerk when she gets back from her chat with the manager (although really she's probably just putting a fresh coat of nail polish on before giving us the brush-off. I know how these things work).

So, Ernio might be our only hope right about now. At this point we don't have time to waste.

"I was wondering if you could help us, Ern. We're doing, um . . . um . . . a scavenger hunt. Yup. For school. And we forget where some of the things we need are. Do you think we could borrow your computer to look them up?"

"Of course. You know the concierge motto." He waits for me to repeat it with him. "In Service through Friendship."

"Follow me," he says. We leave just as the front-desk clerk is returning. She waves desperately in our direction and calls out, "Prince Alex!"

Uh-oh. Guess she *was* Googling and not manicuring. Alex doesn't even break stride as we rush away, and I start chattering loudly about last Thanksgiving, so that Ernio won't notice the clerk calling, "Prince Alex, oh, Prince Alex!" across the marbled lobby.

We trail Ernio into a small, but neat, back office.

"*La mia casa è la sua casa,*" he says. "Or at least 'my computer is your computer.'"

We all smile at him, and I sit down at his desk and reach

for the mouse. Ernio props himself on the desk edge and begins asking "Kristoff" and "Svetlana" how they like their exchange program. When they look at him blankly, he says, "Your names. Chloe said you were classmates, but surely you aren't from New York originally."

Sophie is amazing. Right away she starts charming the socks off Ernio with stories about her "exchange program." For someone who has a private tutor, she sure can talk good middle school. Alex accused us earlier of watching too many movies, but clearly we're not the only ones.

I quickly hit print on the list of penny machines and then, while Ernio is distracted by Sophie, a.k.a. Svetlana, I turn on my phone just long enough to e-mail myself the picture of Ingrid under the table at Serendipity and then log into my e-mail account on Ernio's computer. I print the picture out too. Golden!

I power down my phone again and slide it into the back of Ernio's desk drawer. Just in case it's still traceable even when it's off. Alex slips me his as well and manages to mime behind Ernio's back for Sophie and Pay to pass him theirs. I'll give Sophie mad credit. She gets a gold star in diverting attention.

When the printer finishes spitting pages at us, I cough loudly and push back from the desk. "Wow, Ernio, this was hugely helpful. I bet we win the scavenger hunt for sure now."

"What else is on your list? Anything I can help with? Oh wait, who am I talking to? You don't get to be an amazing junior concierge without being exceedingly resourceful, right, kiddo?"

"Go big or go home," I tell him. Wow, that motto comes in handy in so many instances. Good picking on my part.

Ernio walks us back through the lobby to the front door. We all try to shield our faces without looking obvious about it, just in case the front-desk clerk happens to glance up. Luckily, she's busy helping another guest. I hug Ernio, and we burst back into the bright sunshine.

"Don't be a stranger," Ernio calls, and we wave. I grab Pay's arm and all four of us tear down the stairs, brush past the valets, and duck around the corner.

"Think he suspected anything?" Pay asks.

"I don't think so, thanks to Sophie's chattering. Nice job." I give Sophie a genuine smile, but she just shrugs and looks away. Guess the thaw is over. Must be time for the next ice age. Whatever. Not important. The only thing that matters now is finding Ingrid.

I wave the pieces of paper. "Okay, let's figure out where she'd go. I'm thinking Times Square because there are so many clustered there, but I'm not sure if she'd know that.

At Your Service

This just gives street addresses, and she might not figure out how close together they are."

Alex reads over my shoulder. Which is a little awkward because he has to stand pretty close to do it.

"The USS *Intrepid*, the Children's Museum on Staten Island, Yankee Stadium . . . she could be anywhere by now."

Something clicks into place in my head.

"That's it! Yankee Stadium," I say.

Alex comes around to face me. "What makes you say that?"

"Because we talked about it. I told her that would be the hardest one to get because the machine is inside the stadium, which is only open the few hours a day they give tours to the public. I remember telling her we'd have to rush to get there because the tours mostly take place at lunchtime.

"Subway's this way!" I yell, already breaking into a run. If Ingrid skipped the machine at the Central Park Zoo, she could have a good half-hour head start on us. As we run, I give a brief thought to whether Alex and Sophie will be okay on the subway versus the limos they're more accustomed to, but they aren't protesting as they tear down the stairs behind me.

Thinking about limousines makes me remember Bill. What will he do when he gets back with Frans and finds us missing? I can only hope and pray the three of them decide to try to find us on their own, rather than running back to the hotel. I know Bill would never rat me out to Mr. Whilpers, but he likes Dad as much as everyone else does, so he might be tempted to tell him. Ergh. I can't think about that now. *Just keep moving.*

Pay has her MetroCard out before we reach the bottom of the stairs. "Mom just loaded this with more money last week. Line up behind me and keep passing it back."

We each take our turn with the card and huddle together on the subway platform. Waiting for the train to pull up is torture. I just wish this whole day had a fast-forward button, and we could zoom ahead to the part where we have Ingrid safe and sound back at the St. Michèle.

Something tells me it's not gonna be that simple.

Chapter Twenty

F ollow me," commands Pay, skipping down the
stairs of the elevated subway platform in the Bronx.
Across the street is the House That Jeter Built . . .
the new Yankee Stadium. Otherwise known as Pay's second
home. Yeah, she doesn't just wear her pink Yankees hoodie
for show. The girl is a major superfan. Her Yankees bobble-
head collection is unrivaled. The last thing she does before
she gets into bed every night is hit each one on the top of his
head. Personally, I think it would be weird to go to sleep with
Babe Ruth nodding away at me, but to each her own.

I spare a quick glance over my shoulder to the park where
the old stadium used to be before they tore it down. I'm not
so much into baseball myself, but I did love afternoons there

with Dad. Every so often his contact in the team's special affairs office would send over a pair of box tickets, and Dad would load us up with bags of peanuts and a foam finger and we'd hop on the subway. Back then my hand had felt so little in his big one as we walked up the ramp to our seats. We haven't caught a game in a while, and I've only been a few times with Pay to the new stadium.

I fight back a sudden lump in my throat as I think of my dad, all sweet and trusting. Am I making a huge mistake not calling him right now? Am I being totally selfish to put Ingrid in jeopardy all so I can save face . . . and my job? Will he ever forgive me if we don't find her right away?

We wait for the light to turn so we can cross 161st Street. In my hand I clutch the printout. I've studied it fourteen bajillion times on the ride uptown, so I know the only scrap of information we have is that the penny machine is in front of the team store. Big help. Paisley informs us there are team stores every few gates. With our luck, we're probably going to have to circle the entire stadium.

Except as we approach Gate Six, the sign for one of the team stores is practically shimmering in the sunlight, just beside the Hard Rock Cafe. Could it be that easy? It's a beautiful sight, either way. Progress is progress, and this feels hopeful.

At Your Service

"Guys, over here!" I gesture to the gate, and the others fall in step behind me.

Just through the doors, in between an information booth and the stadium entrance to the team store, I spy a now-familiar-looking machine, with the crank handle in the twelve o'clock position.

"We found it!" I jump up and down in my excitement. Except then I realize that, while we found the penny machine no problem, we didn't find the thing we actually needed to find *at* the penny machine. Or rather, the person. There is no Ingrid in sight.

Even worse, the gates are locked tight.

"What do we do now? We came all the way out here!" Sophie is understandably upset. Alex squeezes her shoulders, but they just slump even farther. "What if she's hurt? Or someone has her? What if she's scared? Or crying?"

Alex looks as helpless as I feel. Pay just looks annoyed that her precious Yankees are failing us. She grabs hold of the metal gate and shakes, like she's rattling prison bars. I turn to tell her that won't do us any good, but as I do, I spot a tiny movement inside the gates, in the shadows far across the concourse, right where the seats begin.

My breathing stops. Could it possibly be?

The silhouette moves again, and I exhale. The person is way too tall to be a nine-year-old girl. But it *is* someone inside of the gates, and that's at least something.

"Hey!" I yell. When everyone else sees where I'm pointing, they all join me in yelling and shaking the bars. "Over here! Please, help us!"

Moving at about one mile an hour, an elderly man in a custodian uniform makes his way over to us and addresses us through the bars.

"Next tour doesn't start for forty minutes."

"We're not here for a tour, sir. We're looking for a little girl. She's lost, and we think she came here," I say, trying to make my eyes like saucers so he'll take extra pity on us.

"Please, she's my sister and we need to find her," Alex adds.

"You kids have any parents?" he asks.

"Yes, sir. We're, uh, we're all searching for her. We split up to, uh, cover more ground. Have you seen this girl?" I grab the picture I printed of Ingrid under the table playing Barbies and smoosh it against the metal bars.

The custodian slips it through to his side and studies it closely. "Well, now, I believe I did see this little one. She was part of the twelve-twenty tour group."

At Your Service

"The twelve-twenty tour? It's only twelve forty now! That means she's still inside the park, then! Please, please, can you let us in? We promise we'll just grab her and go!" I can't keep a giant smile from stretching across my whole face, and I turn to high-five Alex. Pay and Sophie are hugging and squealing. Man, the feeling is even better than walking out the doors on the last day of school.

But the custodian is shaking his head. "She's not here. I guess I should have picked up on something not quite right. Everyone milling about out here, it was hard to tell who belonged to who. I wouldn't have expected a girl that small to be on her own. Opened the gates to let everyone in, and that one goes straight over to that penny machine over there." He points at the machine to his left, but we're so dejected, none of us turn our heads. Is he trying to tell us we missed her by minutes?

"And after the penny machine?" Alex asks. His voice doesn't sound quite right, almost like he's trying to speak over a lump in his throat.

"Must have slipped out. I followed behind the tour for just a bit before I came back to lock the gates back up, and I don't remember seeing her again. Didn't really put that together in my head until just now, or I'd have been more worried. Though she did seem like she could handle herself, that one. Spunky."

He hands the picture back through the bars with a sad smile. "I'm really sorry, kids. I wish I'd been paying more attention. Have you called the police? Need me to make that call for you?"

"Oh no, sir, no need! Um, it's just that, well, our parents already have. Yes, and they're waiting for them. We, uh, we should get back to them so they don't worry they've lost us, too. Heh-heh." My laugh sounds pitiful, and it's completely obvious that I'm lying, but the custodian seems to buy it, because he just gives another tight smile and a little wave as he returns to the concourse.

"Good luck. I have faith!" he calls.

At least someone does. Sophie, on the other hand, looks like she's about to lose it.

"Alex?" she moans. It's just one word, but it's full of panic.

"She's okay, Soph. I feel it in my bones. We just have to get to her. It's all going to be perfectly fine." Alex bends his knees so that his eyes are level with hers, and he puts his thumb under her chin and raises her head to meet them.

"Soph, it's Ingrid we're talking about. Ingrid. She's fine!"

At Your Service

Sophie's smile is halfhearted, but it's definitely there. Then she takes a deep breath, gives a little shake of her hair, lifts her shoulders, and resumes her royal posture. You could never even tell that she'd been about to lose it. Wow. Those must be some amazing princess lessons she's gotten. I need to find me some of those.

I take the printout of locations and slap it up against the limestone wall of the stadium.

"Where to next?" I try not to sound as hopeless as I feel.

"Where would Ingrid go next?" Pay asks.

I study the list. "She'd likely go on to the Bronx Zoo. It's not exactly simple, because it involves some train transfers, but it's the only other place with penny machines in the Bronx, and if you're already out here, it wouldn't make sense to go back to the city only to come back here later. Especially since she wants to get ones from every penny machine on the list, and I told her how many were at the zoo."

I begin to pull the paper back toward me, but Sophie grabs it out of my hands. In a not-very-princess-like manner, I might add.

"What if she isn't headed there? We have no way of knowing she'd go there next."

Alex takes a deep breath. "All right, then, let's read

over the rest of the list and try to think like Ingrid. It's still possible she would have gone to Times Square because so many machines are clustered there."

I may have been tongue-tied in Alex's presence yesterday, but right now I have no trouble forming words. Especially because I'm so sure I'm right and he's wrong.

I say, "But then again, we don't know if she would recognize that those places are all in Times Square, because it just lists them by street address. I'm positive she would have gone from here to the zoo."

Pay makes a tiny noise behind us, like clearing her throat. When we all turn to look at her, she says, "Sorry, guys, but I don't think it's my place to weigh in here. I see a street cart on the corner over there, so I'm gonna grab us a quick lunch. Who knows when we'll get another chance to eat, and we should keep our energy up."

She trots off, and I can't help envying her role in all this. Obviously she completely cares about Ingrid's safety and will stick with us until we find her, but she definitely doesn't have the same things at stake the rest of us do.

Sophie continues to study the list like it's got the secrets to the universe printed on it. "Alex!" She points. "The Empire State Building is on here."

At Your Service

Alex leans in close to see. "That has to be it. Ingrid *loves* the Empire State Building."

See, now these are the kind of things it would be nice to share with your friendly concierge. I didn't even have it on my list of planned activities because I had us seeing bird's-eye views of the city from the Top of the Rock instead. I mean, totally beside the point right now, of course, but I'm just saying.

A minute later Pay jogs back to us, juggling two hot dogs in each hand, and passes them out. Alex finishes his in two bites and looks a little wistfully at his empty napkin. Sophie, on the other hand, takes dainty nibbles, dabbing at the corners of her mouth with her napkin between each bite. I eat mine like a normal person.

"I still think the Bronx Zoo makes more logical sense." I'm not giving up without a fight.

"Know many nine-year-olds who think logically, do you?" Alex asks with that annoying—no, adorable—no, definitely annoying eyebrow lift. But he has a point. Sort of.

"What if we split up?" Pay asks, but before the words are even out of her mouth, I'm shaking my head.

"Definitely not. Not even an option. Why don't we take a vote for where we go next? All for Bronx Zoo?"

I raise my hand. Paisley hesitates and I'm waiting for another "it's not my place" speech, but then she takes one look at me and her hand shoots up. I reply with a grateful smile. Alex and Sophie jam their hands down by their side.

"So we're tied. And I believe the guest is never wrong, therefore we'll be going to the Empire State Building." Sophie sounds smug. Oh no she didn't! Did they just pull the "I'm the guest and you're the employee" card?

She *knows* I can't argue with that one. ERGH!

I grab Pay's arm and turn my back on both royals. I assume they're following as we make our way to the subway platform, but I don't bother turning around to check. At this point I don't even know whether to scream or cry. All I know is that this day is not going AT ALL the way I planned it on my tidy little to-do list. And I even used my matching pen to write it, like the composed and professional hotel employee I am.

So not fair.

Chapter Twenty-One

The air outside might be warm(ish), but the subway ride back to the city is completely frosty. As in Arctic.

By the time we snag four seats across from one another in a mostly empty car, we are sweaty and tired and three-quarters of us are still hungry. I'm leaving Sophie out because she barely finished her hot dog to begin with. Maybe princesses don't need to eat the way regular people do.

"Do we change trains?" Sophie asks, breaking the silence, as we rumble through the lower Bronx.

"No, this will take us to Herald Square. It's only a few blocks to the Empire State Building from there," Pay answers from her seat next to me.

Sophie whispers something in Alex's ear, and his eyes flick up, land on me, then dart around, before lowering again. Are they talking about me? Okay, so she could be pointing out the guy with purple and red dreadlocks in the seat just down from us, but somehow it feels like them against us. Or actually them against me, since, even though she voted with me, we all know Pay is as neutral as Switzerland.

"So, what do you guys think of New York so far? I mean, outside of the reason we're seeing so much of it right now." I have to give Pay credit. She really is trying to smooth things over.

"I'm sorry, but if you really want to know, I think it's smelly and dirty and the people are rude and it's too loud," says Sophie.

Seriously? I'm sorry, but does she not have the slightest clue how special this city is? Does she think Frank Sinatra would "start spreading the news" about the worst place ever? Does she imagine people would leave everything and come here with, like, a hundred dollars in their pocket and a dream of making it big if it was such a horrible place? Has she not seen all the T-shirts? They don't say I FROWNY-FACE NY. No. They say I HEART NY. And anyone who doesn't heart it themselves must not have a heart to begin with.

I take my glasses off and begin cleaning them furiously

with the edge of my shirt. I guess I mutter under my breath a little too.

"Pardon? Did you have something you wanted to say, Chloe?" Sophie's voice is as chilly as the inside of the ice machines on every floor of my hotel. For someone who was so intent on avoiding conflict earlier today, she sure seems to be looking for a fight now.

And she's gonna get one.

"Just that maybe you shouldn't trash someone else's hometown right in front of them. I would think a queen-in-training might have been taught a little diplomacy."

"Pardon me? Shows what you know. Alex will be king, and his daughter would be the next queen. Not me." She seems smug, but I don't see why. That just means she's already achieved the pinnacle of her job titles already, which I find pretty depressing.

"If New York City is so terrible, what is it about Somerstein that's sooo wonderful, *Princess* Sophie?"

She shifts in her seat to glare at me. Her voice might be cool, but her eyes are shooting white-hot laser beams of hate at me. "Will you *please* quit it with the Princess Sophie stuff? How is it that from the very first instant she met us this morning Paisley has recognized that we *only* want to be treated like regular, normal people, and yet you still haven't? We don't *want* to push in the queue to get our seats at restaurants. We don't *need* an 'educational and thoughtful' itinerary delivered by some business-suited hotel robot-girl. And we definitely don't enjoy being addressed by titles all day, especially by someone who's our age. Do you not think that makes us feel ridiculous?"

I open and close my mouth a few times, but I can't find the words I want to say. Like how I was just doing MY JOB. Or trying to anyway. I stare wide-eyed at her for another second, and then I get up and march to the opposite end of the subway car.

When I'm plopped in my new seat, I unclip my barrette and let my hair fall over my face. Pay makes a move to come after me, but then Alex grabs her arm and stops her. Instead he stands and works his way toward me as Paisley drops down next to Sophie. He has to use the handrails above him for balance while the train car sways back and forth, since he doesn't have "subway legs" like I do.

"Pardon me, miss. Is this seat taken?" Alex asks when he reaches me. So cheesy. But it works. I allow a tiny smile and gesture for him to sit down. He does, then leans back in his seat and sticks his long legs out into the aisle. They stretch toward the bench of seats across from us.

At Your Service

"Sorry about Sophie," Alex says, not looking at me.

The words hang in the air for a minute, because I don't want to just let her off the hook so easily. Then again, it's not Alex I'm mad at, at least not at this exact moment. Not really. He might be really arrogant, and I haven't always understood his behavior today. But he hasn't been actively rude about my city, like his sister. And the way he's been comforting Sophie and standing back to let us pass through doors first and helping brainstorm our plans (even if he never agrees with me) and stuff has actually been sort of . . . princely. But in a good prince way, not a jerky "ooh, get a load of me, I'm a prince" way. So maybe he's more cocky than arrogant after all. Trust me, there's a difference.

But still. For a second I wish I could go back to the days when my biggest worry was making Marie LaFou crack a smile. I'd thought *that* was achieving the impossible, when really it was a walk in Central Park compared to these guys. I let myself indulge in a little fantasy where Sophie's face is lined up directly across from the Rockettes when they start their kickline.

When I don't answer, Alex puts his hand on my knee. Well, THAT sure snaps me back to reality. His palm feels warm even through the fabric of my pants, and now the kickline moves into my belly.

"Really she just didn't want to answer that question about Somerstein. Then she'd be forced to tell you what our number one claim to fame is." Alex's voice is low and close and it makes me shiver, which is weird since it's also as warm as his hand.

I shouldn't give in so easily, but I'm curious. "Which is?"

"We're the world's largest producer of false teeth."

I can't help it. I burst out laughing. "WHAT?!"

"Indeed. I'm serious. You can Google it. We're also the largest producers of sausage casings."*

"Okay, I thought I knew a lot of weird New York facts, but I got nothin' to top that one."

"What have you got?"

I think for a second.

"Um, well, we don't have a Main Street in Manhattan, but Broadway, which starts downtown and goes all the way to Albany, is one of the longest streets in the world."

"Not bad. Not better than false teeth, but not terrible. Incidentally, that means Broadway is way longer than my entire country."

"Is your country longer than a hundred and fifty miles? 'Cuz that's how long Broadway is."

---

* Wonder if this explains Sophie's distaste for her hot dog. It's all becoming clearer now.

At Your Service

"Measured north to south we're twenty-four kilometers long."

"Um, in miles please?"

"Do they not teach you anything in your schools here? Twenty-four kilometers is about fifteen miles, give or take."

"Oh yeah. Then Broadway's definitely longer."

"False teeth," he reminds me. He does have a point. You can't out-weird that one.

"Oh, okay, how about this one?" I say. "We have Manhattanhenge twice a year."

"What on earth is Manhattanhenge? Is that like Mardi Gras?"

I laugh. "No, it's like Stonehenge in England, where the rocks are in a circle and it's supposed to mean something astrological or astronomical or whatever. Two days a year the sunset lines up with the grid pattern of our streets. When the sun sets, it shines exactly in the center line of every east-west street in the city."

"All right, that's quite impressive."

"Cooler than false teeth?" I tease.

"Could be close." Alex shifts in his seat and faces me just a little. "Seriously though, Sophie doesn't usually explode like that. She's very much in control of her emotions under ordinary circumstances. She's just not herself today. Understandably."

I sigh. I know he's right (I've seen her manners on display), and I should cut her some slack. Her sister is running around all alone in a city that I might love, but that probably seems enormous and scary to someone who comes from somewhere so small.

I keep my voice quiet as I say, "It's not like me to talk to a guest like that either, so I get it. I think we're all pretty stressed. I can't stop thinking about my dad and wondering if we made the right decision not to let the adults handle things."

Alex draws his legs in and hugs them to his chest. "Me too."

I sneak a glance at him. "What's your dad like? Is he going to freak?"

Alex slides down a little in his seat. "Fantastically. At home he's really brilliant about Ingrid taking off. I think he finds it impressive the way she's so eager to get outside and explore. He says he was the same way when he was small and seeing the world has helped him immensely as a king. To be honest, I've always been a bit jealous of the way he is with her. I just wonder sometimes . . ."

I wait for him to finish, but he doesn't. I prod him with a gentle, "Wonder what?"

"If he thinks she'd make a better successor than me. I'm quite an ordinary lad with ordinary-lad interests. I don't think he considers a passion for football—er, soccer—and video games to be a great mark of a leader or anything. He says I need more structure and responsibility to learn to take my future role seriously. Hence, all his talk about military school. I only want him to see that I do take it seriously and that I can lead when I need to. It's more that I don't get an awful lot of chances to show him."

I swivel in my seat to face Alex. I should be freaking out at how close our legs are and how my shoulder bumps against his every time the subway car lurches, but everything he's saying is exactly how I feel and I just need to tell him.

"It's like that with me, too. I mean, it's not like I'm in line for a crown, but more than anything I want to follow in my dad's footsteps and be a concierge and help people. I guess making sure someone has an unforgettable trip isn't exactly as import-ant as being a world leader or whatever, but I love how people light up when they get to do something extra special and that makes me feel really good. I like making people happy. Plus, I really want my dad to see that I can be just as good at it as he is. I *thought* I was doing that, but after today . . ."

Alex nods glumly. "After today, we could both be in the rubbish bin. And I could be shipping off to learn preci-sion drills and boot-camp marches and, well, whatever else happens at military school. Even if Ingrid is safe and sound at the hotel eating bonbons in the bathtub right now."

Wow, I hadn't even considered that she might have just gone back to the hotel. But I don't have time to ponder that one because just then a couple things happen at the same time:

A. The announcement comes on that our stop is next.

B. Alex reaches over and holds my hand.

C. Is there even any thought of a C after I just said what I said for B?!

He looks at my shocked expression and smiles.

"You're quite different than I imagined, Chloe. We have a lot more in common than I expected."

We . . . we . . . we do? I am? Wait, what's my name again? My brain is a jumble of thoughts that make no sense, like when the orchestra warms up before a Broadway show and it's all just a bunch of noises that tumble on top of one another.

Alex straightens in his seat. "Is this our stop? You said Herald Square?"

It hasn't even been a full minute of hand holding. Crud! Alex unlaces his fingers from mine and struggles to his feet as the car jolts underneath him. I struggle too, even though I've long since perfected the art of standing on a moving subway train. More like my legs are wobblier than an overcooked piece of Little Italy fettuccini due to the fact that he just held my hand. On PURPOSE.

The train jerks to a stop and the doors slide open. I am in my own little floaty bubble high above the earth as I let go of the handrail and step off the train. So much in my own bubble universe that, for the first time in an entire lifetime of riding the subway, I forget to do the one thing the announcements are always telling people to do: "Watch your step as you exit the train." I turn at the last second to make sure Pay and Sophie are getting off through the other set of doors farther down the car, and as I swish back, the doors slide closed.

On me. Or, more specifically, on my purse, which is slung diagonally across my back. The doors open back up, but it's too late. I've lost my balance and that's all it takes.

I go down hard.

Chapter Twenty-Two

Someone screams. No, wait, I think that's me.

I scream.

I'm sprawled on my knees on the bumpy yellow warning strip of the platform, which kills to kneel on. My ankle is throbbing beyond belief and I go dizzy from the pain.

Ahead of me, Alex stops and pivots in place. He spots me immediately and his eyes go wide.

He takes three steps to reach me, and they look like the giant steps we used to attempt when we played Mother, May I? in the recess yard at school. Probably because everything is moving so super slow.

He bends down and his arms go under my armpits, but I yelp in pain when my ankle bumps against the cement subway platform. Sophie and Paisley rush over.

"Chlo, omigosh, are you okay?" Pay asks.

I sort of half answer/half whimper a tiny yes, but my ankle is growing ten sizes bigger with every passing second. Around us, people are sympathetic, but not so much that they aren't still trying to get past me to board the next train.

Alex has a little frown line between his eyes as he looks around, then down at me. "Okay, Chloe. I'm going to carry you over to the bench over there, but I don't want to jostle your ankle too much. Do you trust me?"

I think of his hand warm in mine a few minutes ago and give him a nod.

"Put your arms around my neck."

He leans down next to me and I follow his instructions. He puts one of his arms around my back and the other underneath my legs and stands, cradling me against him.

Okay, my ankle might be screeching worse than the brakes of the PATH train pulling onto the tracks above us, but holy wow! Swept off my feet and carried away—literally—by the handsome prince. Granted, in the fairy tales the damsel in distress does not have a purplish-black bruise forming on her ankle that looks scarier than that Naked Cowboy guy who wanders Times Square in nothing but his underwear, boots, and a ten-gallon hat. But still. Gotta grab the fairy tale where you can get it.

"Okay?" Alex asks, and I manage a squeaky yes. There's a knot in my throat equally as big as the one on my ankle.

I nod again and bury my face in his shoulder. He walks carefully to the far side of the station where there are benches, and I try to distract myself from the pulsing pain by trying to figure out what brand of laundry detergent his maids use to make his sweater smell so amazing.

Alex settles me gently on a bench. A twenty-something guy wearing a rumpled black T-shirt and grungy jeans jumps up so there's room to prop my leg.

"Whoa. Dudes, that was like a rad scene right there," says the guy. He peers around the guitar slung over his shoulder. "Are you okay?"

Before I can answer, an NYPD officer is standing in front of us. "Are you all right, miss? I saw what happened and I'll have an ambulance here in just a few minutes."

"No!" I scream. An ambulance means hospitals and paperwork and . . . Dad. All three things that will make finding Ingrid a statistical improbability. No can do. Not today.

"I think it's just twisted," I say, reaching forward and

rubbing at my throbbing ankle. It pounds like it has its own heartbeat. Thud, thud, thud.

Pay and Alex lean over me. Sophie is just behind Paisley, biting her lip feverishly. I bet she regrets her last words to me now. Serves her right.

"Chloe, don't be an idiot. If you need the hospital, we'll get you there," Pay says. Then she drops her voice to a whisper so the officer won't hear her. "Alex and Sophie can keep looking for Ingrid, and I'll stay with you." Her eyes are filled with concern.

I glance at the policeman, but he's preoccupied with his radio. "It would take them twice as long. They don't know their way around the city. I'm okay. Mostly."

"How is it not going to take twice as long with you in no condition to walk?" Pay has a pretty good argument there.

"We need to stay together." I feel like a crusty old army sergeant in the middle of a bloody battle: *I'm not leaving my men!* But really, I'm not. We may be having the day from Hell-o Kitty, but I'm not ready to stop looking now. Even if my ankle is starting to swell so bad, it might need its own zip code soon.

The officer finishes talking into his radio and bends down to talk to me face-to-face. "What's your name, sweetheart?"

I can't seem to make his words compute, so Paisley answers for me. "It's Chloe."

He smiles. "Okay, Chloe. I imagine that's a bit of a scare you just had, so you're probably going to feel a little strange for a bit. I'm Officer O'Brien and I can help. Do you want to give me the name and number of a parent or guardian? And then we'll get you some medical attention and fill out a bit of paperwork."

I swallow. This. Totally. Sucks. Now that the shock is starting to wear off, the reality of what just happened sets in. I start to shake a bit and then a bit more. Alex maneuvers onto the bench next to me and his arm comes around me. I know this is the same thing he did with Sophie in front of Yankee Stadium, so this is just how he comforts, but omigosh a cute boy has his arm around me and that's all kinds of weird.

"How about that number?" Officer O'Brien asks.

"Um, could you give us just a few minutes with Chloe, Officer?" Pay's voice sounds confident now, even though I know her well enough to know she's faking it.

He looks confused. "Sure. I guess. But the ambulance is on its way. I'll just . . . . I'll just head up to the street to direct them. Be right back."

"Okay, Chloe. What are our options here?" Pay asks, the second the cop is out of earshot.

"We need to make a run for it, but obviously that's pretty impossible for me."

"It's not if I carry you." Alex's voice sounds confident too, but I definitely don't know him well enough to know if he's faking it or not. It didn't seem like any effort for him to pick me up and get me to the bench, but we're talking about a way longer distance now.

Sophie decides to join in finally. "He can, too. He plays an awful lot of polo and you should see him swing a mallet. He's really strong."

I hesitate. I'm fairly light. It could work. "It might be easier if we try piggyback. If you can use your hands to keep my knees close to your side, so my ankle doesn't move too much, I think you could go a lot faster than carrying me the other way."

Much as I didn't mind being swooped up by the handsome prince for those thirty seconds.

"We'd have to go now. Like, right now," Paisley says.

"You kids are major baddies," says the guitar player, who is still standing next to us. "I approve!"

Gee, thanks. Now that we have *his* approval, we're all set.

Pay grabs a five from her wallet and tosses it into his open guitar case on the floor.

"That's for sending Officer O'Brien in the opposite direction when he gets back."

"Rock on," he answers.

Alex crouches in front of me. He looks a bit uncertain, but he says, "Ready? Tell me if it hurts too much. If it does, we're abandoning this idea right away, getting you help, and calling our parents. It's not worth it."

All I can manage is a nod. I want to scream with the pain of it, but I align myself with his back and put my hands on his shoulders.

We have to head for the far exit so we don't surface in the same spot as Officer O'Brien. As we speed-walk up the steps, the guy with the guitar starts playing, and I recognize the lyrics from an old Sheryl Crow CD in Mom's acoustic collection.

"So run, baby, run, baby, run, baby, run, baby, run . . ."

I turn my face into Alex's shoulder and giggle through the pain.

Then I pick up my head to ask, "Hey, did you know that musicians who play in New York subways have to go through a really intense audition process to be allowed a spot on a platform? Some of them have even played at Carnegie Hall."

At Your Service

Alex is starting to breathe a little heavy from carrying me up so many stairs, but he manages a chuckle.

"It's nice to know you feel well enough to work the trivia, Chlo."

Chlo. Usually only Dad and Pay call me that, but I never, ever get goose bumps on my arm when *they* say it.

I snuggle back into his shoulder. There's a lot about today that's been monumentally bad, but one or two moments have been just perfect.

Chapter Twenty-Three

As soon as we're at street level, I direct Alex toward Thirty-Third Street and into Greeley Square. It's just a small little triangle of a park where Broadway meets Sixth Avenue, but we can hide out in here and Alex can rest. He deposits me carefully at an umbrellaed café table. We're getting our first stretch of true spring weather, and the weekend crowds hide us perfectly.

Very close by, I hear an ambulance siren cut off as it reaches its destination, and I swallow. I was just a baby when 9/11 happened, but even I know that firemen, policemen, and EMTs are rock stars in New York City, and I feel totally terrible that we just ran out on so many people taking the time to try to help me. It could possibly be illegal, even though it wasn't *my* idea to call the ambulance.

I swallow and try to push it to the back corner of my mind, right alongside the worry over Ingrid, as we wait for Sophie and Pay, who kept going when we turned into the park. They're on the hunt for a Duane Reade so they can grab some basic medical supplies for me. I'm hoping they consider horse tranquilizer "basic" because I could sure go for anything that will make this throbbing pain ease up.

They should be back any second. It's pretty hard to walk a whole city block in Manhattan without encountering a Duane Reade. I swear, there are probably more of them than taxicabs in this town. While we wait, Alex finds me a small paper cup of water from the sandwich kiosk in the square.

"Sorry, I couldn't get more than this. They kept trying to sell me a bottled water, even though I told them I had no money."

I snap my head up at this. The guy's dad is worth billions-with-a-capital-B, and he doesn't have any money? He could buy Herald Square, if he wanted. Now I'm definitely distracted from my pain.

"You have *no* money? As in zero?"

He stands and makes a show of turning his pockets inside out for me. A small piece of dryer lint flutters to the ground.

"Never really been an issue before now," he says. He looks almost embarrassed.

Oh. Oh, I get it. Why would a prince need to carry money? What could he want in his own country that someone wouldn't just hand him? Sure, maybe they'd bill his dad later or something, but probably not even. And when he travels, he has his bodyguards and Elise and, well, people like me. I certainly wouldn't have allowed him to pay for anything all day, if we'd still been out doing the tourist thing.

But then, that means . . .

"I don't suppose Sophie has any money on her either, then, huh?"

Alex sits back down. "Wouldn't reckon."

And Ingrid has *my* wallet. So unless Pay came into a surprise inheritance between now and the last time we hung out, when her personal fortune included about sixty bucks in birthday money, we could be in a little bit of trouble here. Correction, a little bit *more* trouble. Because, sure, why not? This day hasn't been quite sucky enough yet with a lost guest, another with a total attitude, and . . . what am I forgetting here? Oh, right, an ankle the size of Grand Central Station!

Paisley and Sophie appear on the park walkway and wave in our direction. Alex waves back. I would too, if I felt like I had any reason to be perky. Pain coupled with broke status makes me cranky, turns out.

"Hey, guys. How you doing, Chlo? Hopefully this stuff we got will help." Pay tosses a bag on the table and reaches down to squeeze my hand. Sophie is still not quite making eye contact. Fine by me. Let her keep feeling guilty for her rotten words.

"We have an Ace bandage to wrap your ankle, extra-strength pain reliever, and an energy bar, so you don't have to take the medicine on a mostly empty stomach," Pay announces, unpacking the bag onto the table.

No horse tranquilizer, but totally practical supplies. Pay is super good in a crisis.

Except, as great as this stuff she bought is, it cost money we don't have. Couple that with the hot dogs at the stadium and the five she just tossed Guitar Guy, and I'm guessing we are just about at the end of Paisley's birthday money fund.

"Um, so, Pay, just save the receipt, so I can reimburse you when we get back to the hotel." I try to make my voice all casual sounding. "Incidentally, how much money do you have left, exactly?"

"Well, Mom gave me some cash for today, so I wouldn't be expecting the hotel to cover my stuff. I have . . ." She flips through bills in her wallet. "Twenty-seven dollars. Plus a bunch of change."

Twenty-seven dollars. That is not so much. Not in New York City money anyway. Things here always cost more than they do everywhere else. But, if we're careful, maybe we can make it stretch. If we can find Ingrid at the Empire State Building, we'll definitely be able to make it work, but if our wild-goose chase goes on much longer, I don't know. Hopefully, Pay's subway card has enough on it so it can keep covering our fares. I can't imagine Alex will be able to carry me too far.

Honestly, is the universe trying to send us a sign? I peer up at the sky, like I expect to see the bat signal or something. Or maybe one of those skywriting airplanes scrawling, *Chloe, just call home.*

But all I see are a few puffy clouds and the tip-tops of buildings, including the spire of the Empire State Building, where we're headed next.

Alex fills Paisley and Sophie in on our dwindling funds situation while he wraps my ankle. Not gonna lie. I can barely feel anything beyond the throbbing in my foot, but when Alex props my leg on his knee and cradles my ankle in his hand, it feels a lot more tingly than sharp, splitting pain-y.

At Your Service

"Hey, so where'd you learn how to do this?" I'm thinking a prince probably doesn't have to spend much time practicing first aid.

"I'm quite hands-on with our polo ponies. Once you've wrapped a Thoroughbred's leg, a girl's ankle is quite simple. And as a bonus, you aren't likely to crush me under you if I bungle things."

Probably not.

Anyway, it helps. I scarf down the PowerBar and swallow the maximum dose of pills it says on the bottle and, with my ankle wrapped tight, I feel pretty okay(ish). I still don't want to put too much pressure on it, but it's bearable to hobble along.

"I'll hang back with Chloe, if you girls want to run ahead to the building," Alex offers. I'm not sure if he's a prince or my knight in shining armor, but either way, I'll take it. He smiles at my grateful grin. "What, did you think we were just going to leave you behind?"

"It might make more sense."

"Don't be daft. You're too much a part of the group. Come on, Gimpy."

Hmm . . . I definitely prefer Chlo.

Chapter Twenty-Four

Paisley and Sophie backtrack to intercept us as Alex and I round the corner of Thirty-Third onto Fifth Avenue.

"Bad news. The guy at the information desk inside says the penny machines were taken out of the lobby, but he isn't sure if they're gone or if they've just been moved. They could be out of service or they could be up on the observation level. And no one else has asked about them today. I checked."

"So we need to go up, then?" Alex asks.

"Well, that's just it. It costs twenty-seven dollars to go up there." Paisley looks like the Yankees just lost the World Series.

"That's the kid's price?" I ask. See? New York equals megabucks.

At Your Service

"No, the kid's price is twenty-one, but it's only for twelve and under."

Sophie hesitates, then raises her hand. "I'm twelve."

We all turn to look at her. Of the four of us, I'd choose any one of us over her to send up there alone. Not that she isn't capable . . . probably . . . but, unlike Paisley, she's definitely not so good in a crisis. And if she gets up there and doesn't find Ingrid, who's to say she doesn't lose it eighty-six stories up in the sky, with none of us there to comfort her?

Then again, having six dollars to our name is somehow more reassuring than having zero, and I feel like any of the rest of us lying about our age would just be bad karma. We don't need that right now.

"It's a plan," I say. Alex and Paisley nod too.

Please, please, please, PLEASE let Ingrid be there. I've been able to pretty much shut out worry about her and stay focused on how we're sure to find her, but it's been over two hours now and that's a lot of time for a little girl to be missing in a city this size. We have to find her here. We just *have* to.

When Sophie steps off the elevator exactly twenty-three minutes later, she looks dazed. Actually, she looks like I must have when Alex took my hand on the subway. Too bad he hasn't tried any more of that, but I'm guessing the fact that Pay is with us has kept him from making any moves.

Which isn't to say he hasn't been totally adorable, because he has. He tried to kill time by showing us how he can juggle, using our shoes. Or maybe I'm just finding it hard to see anything he does or says as the least bit less than perfect because I'm seeing him in such a new light.

Amazing. I'm not even worried about the professional ramifications of falling for a hotel guest anymore. I think we're all way past worrying about trivial stuff like that. Whoa. Did *I* just say that? Except, I don't have time to think about my love life *or* my career right now. Sophie isn't dragging a little sister behind her, and that's bad.

She plops down beside us. "No machines," she says. "I did the whole loop of the observation deck inside and out and showed her picture to a slew of the guards up there. No one has seen a penny machine or Ingrid."

So Ingrid is still out there somewhere, and we have no clues left now.

"If you didn't find out anything about Ingrid, how come you look all loony?" Alex asks the same question I want to.

"Oh—um—well, it's just that . . . Uh, I think I might owe you an apology, Chloe."

At Your Service

What? Did I sprain my ears along with my ankle? Because it sounds like the Ice Princess just said something about an apology, but surely my hearing isn't working right. I cock my head and examine her. She looks me straight in the eye. Points to her for that.

"It's only that, well, I *was* looking so hard for Ingrid, I swear. But I couldn't help glancing out at the views a couple of times and . . ."

We all wait for her to continue.

"And it was beautiful! I mean really, really breathtaking. I know we have the Alps and all the ancient buildings around us, and they're quite amazing too, but this was just so . . . so . . ." She throws her hands up. "And the skyline goes on *for ages*!"

AHA! I knew it! I knew it, I knew it, I knew it. You give me the biggest NYC hater on the planet, and somewhere, somehow I WILL find something to change her mind. Okay, granted, this wasn't really my own doing, but so what? I knew it! I want to do a little happy dance, but it would have to be a one-legged jig and I don't know any of those.

"It is pretty special," I say, all demurelike. I can afford to be modest now that I've won my case. But inside I'm still rocking a ginormous *Ha-ha, I told you so!*

Mission accomplished. Just happened to be the wrong mission.

Paisley brings me crashing back to reality. "What now?" she asks.

I tug out the list of penny machines again and spread it out on the floor in front of us. It's fairly crumpled by now.

Alex studies the paper. "Well, I imagine at this point we need to start playing the odds. Times Square has six machines and it's the closest to us, so it makes sense to go there next. I know you didn't want to, Chlo, but if we split up, we can cover a lot more ground."

"I don't know. With Chloe in her condition . . ." Paisley jumps to my defense.

"That's partly the reason we need to. We can't make her walk all over, and I don't want to leave her alone. Soph, maybe you should stay with Paisley since she knows the area." Alex examines the list. "If you girls can take the Toys 'R' Us, M&M's World, Bubba Gump's, and Ellen's Stardust Diner, Chloe and I can visit Madame Tussauds wax museum and Ripley's Believe It or Not! The addresses are right next to each other, so it shouldn't be too much walking for Chloe. And Chlo, I *can* carry you if you need me to."

I turn the bright red color of the TKTS booth that sells

half-price tickets to Broadway shows. Being carried up the subway stairs is one thing, but riding piggyback through a swarm of gawking tourists in Times Square would feel totally ridiculous. Then again, there *is* the Naked Cowboy there and about forty bajillion flashing lights and TV screens. Probably no one would even notice us.

"We'll see. I think I'm okay hopping if I can lean on your arm again. I can tell the medicine is starting to kick in, and it's wrapped so tight, it really doesn't hurt to put a little pressure on it."

"You're quite brave," Alex says, and his eyes lock on mine. We have a total moment.

Yikes, I hope Paisley and Sophie aren't paying attention. So embarrassing. Still, no chance I'm looking away first. He finally smiles his lopsided grin and drops his eyes. Whew. My heart starts back up.

The girls seem oblivious, thank goodness. They're comparing the list to a fold-out city map Paisley snagged from an information desk and circling the locations of Times Square penny machines.

"Okay, let's get a move on. Should we walk or take the subway?" Pay asks when they finish. She looks to me for an answer.

"Walk. By the time we get back to the station and down to the platforms and then back up at Forty-Second Street, it's probably just as much walking as sticking to the streets. Plus, we won't have to worry about encountering Officer O'Brien."

The four of us take off at a decent pace up Fifth Avenue, sticking together long enough to stop at a copy center and make another flyer of Ingrid's photo, so each set of us will have one to show around. Five dollars and thirty-five cents left.

When we get to the New York Public Library, we turn left and cut through Bryant Park, where Alex and I wish luck to Paisley and Sophie. They're headed up to Fifty-First Street to Ellen's Stardust Diner. Then they'll loop back to Times Square to hit the other spots and meet up with us.

Paisley says, "Okay, forty-five minutes, in front of Gap. Sound good?"

"Oh, I love Gap!" says Sophie.

I hang my head. Of course she does. Most down-to-earth royals EVER.

Chapter Twenty-Five

Alex gestures to his back. "Your chariot awaits."

"You're not allowed to make that joke if you actually own a chariot, you know." But I'm too tired to protest, and I know we'll move much faster this way.

"Are you sure you're all right with this?"

"It's fine. No sweat."

Le sigh. He really is a prince. Fortunately, it's only a couple blocks before we get there, though the crush of tourists gawking at all the pretty, pretty lights slows us down a lot.

Madame Tussauds wax museum is usually a super-fun place. Dad had a guest a couple of years ago who wanted to see behind the scenes, so I got to go with them to watch how they make the molds for the wax figures. It was seriously wild. Someone's actual *job* is threading every single piece of hair into the wax head, and someone else hand paints all the eyeballs. Imagine *that* phone conversation with her parents: "Mom, I got a job today! I know, I know. I'm really excited. I'm going to be painting celebrity eyeballs. What? No, I didn't hit my head."

The outside of the museum is pretty outrageous too—all red and gold with this spaceship-looking silver thing as an awning at the opening and a creepy-looking giant sculpted hand holding the MADAME TUSSAUDS sign. As if otherwise you might not know you were at a wax museum.

Only today there's a huge crowd blocking the entrance, and red velvet ropes are keeping everyone out.

Figures.

We're at a standstill anyway, so I slide off Alex's back, making sure to land on my good foot.

"Hey, what's going on here?" I ask the frizzy-haired woman standing next to us. We're still a good distance down the sidewalk, but I assume she knows something because she has an autograph book and pen in her hand, and she's on tiptoes trying to see over the top of everyone's heads.

"They're unveiling Ben Matthews's wax figure."

"The basketball star?" Duh. I mean, how many other Ben

At Your Service

Matthews famous enough to be in a wax museum are there in the world, but it just sort of tumbles out.

The woman snorts. "Yeah."

Well, she doesn't have to be rude about it. I *was* going to be helpful and tell her she won't need to be on tiptoes to see him, since he's seven-foot-something and pretty unmissable, but now . . . *pfft.*

Besides, I have more important things to worry about. People keep pushing against me. It's only a matter of time before someone steps on my foot or jostles my ankle, and I cannot be held accountable for my actions when that happens. Plus, if we can't get through, it's not looking likely that Ingrid could have fought her way to the front *and* talked her way under the ropes.

"How long have people been lined up?" I ask Frizz.

"I got here Thursday."

O-kaaaaay. Really? Just to see a basketball player walk a red carpet? Call me crazy, but wouldn't tickets to a Knicks game get her just as close to him? I know those stadium seats aren't all that comfy, but compared to a Manhattan sidewalk for two days? Plus, the stadium is heated. And there are nachos.

Well, whatever. She answered my question. If this crowd

has been here that long, Ingrid definitely wouldn't have been able to get any penny from Madame Tussauds. Now we just need to find a way around it, so we can check out the scene at Ripley's Believe It or Not! It's right next door, but I definitely don't think my ankle can handle crowds like this. We're better off crossing the street, going down a bit, and coming at it from the other direction.

I lean in to tell my plan to Alex, but the sudden roar of the crowd makes that impossible. A limo has stopped in front of the red carpet. I can't see much over the top of the crowd, but sure enough, a second later there's a head bobbing along a full foot above everyone else, and Ben Matthews smiles at his fans. About a thousand flashes go off. The other entire side of the red carpet must be lined with professional photographers.

In less than five minutes, Ben is inside and it's over. Frizz pushed forward the minute Ben appeared, and I hope she at least got her autograph after all that waiting.

The crowd starts to break up, so I lean on Alex as we move against the stream of fans.

"Have you been in there before?" Alex asks, gesturing at the museum.

"Yeah. You? I know not here, but anywhere?"

"Once. We went to the unveiling of Mom's wax likeness at

At Your Service

Madame Tussauds in London, but we skipped out on Dad's."

Of course. Of course his parents are *in* the museum. And he probably will be too one day. That must feel so weird, to know a whole bunch of strangers are going to pose for pictures with your waxy likeness. Eww. Someone's going to paint his eyeballs someday. Not that they'll ever capture the right shade of navy.

Well, anyway, it's a good reality check. We may have had a "moment" (I don't know, did we? Felt like it, but maybe he holds girls' hands everywhere he goes), but we are living in two totally different worlds. At the very least I should just appreciate that, as much as I love handling things and being the one in charge of my guests, sometimes it's nice to have someone else to lean on, and Alex has been great about that this afternoon.

I let my grip on his arm slip a little, but then my ankle kills, so I grab tight again and hop along next to him. His arm comes around my shoulders to help hold me up. I'm sure he's just being nice. Different worlds and all.

We have to hobble into the street to get around the velvet ropes blocking the museum entrance. Even though I know I'm not going to see Ingrid, I can't help but steal a few peeks at the doors, just in case. But there are only a few official-looking people with walkie-talkies clipped to their · waists moving the rope line. I don't even spot the penny machine, much less Ingrid.

Luckily, Ripley's is right next door. They even share a wall. I'm really grateful Alex claimed these locations for us, because I know Sophie and Paisley have a lot more walking to do, and my ankle is just about shot. I feel bad asking him, but I'm gonna have to ride piggyback to our meeting spot, no doubt about it.

Alex's voice is in my ear. "Ah, Chloe. Don't look now, but I think we've picked up a parasite."

I fake stumble (not easy on a twisted ankle) and look back as if I'm trying to figure out what tripped me. As I ever-so-casually raise my head, I'm greeted by a camera flash right in my face.

The heck?

Chapter Twenty-Six

Alex tugs my arm and orders through clenched teeth, "Turn back around!"

"Ow! I might be blind now! Who's taking my picture?"

"I think it's one of the paparazzi from the wax museum. He must have recognized me."

We've crisscrossed the city all day long without so much as a hint of a photographer or a single autograph request. The woman at the Plaza hadn't even recognized Alex when he'd outright given her his (ridiculously long) name.

Now? Now he gets spotted? Great. We have to meet the girls in twenty-two minutes, and we haven't even checked out Ripley's yet. The last thing we need at this point is a tagalong.

"Just stay close to me," Alex says. Like he has to ask twice on that one.

"Do you get this a lot?" I whisper.

"At home, yes. Outside of Europe, far less. Especially when we're not with Dad. But a little more in the last year, I suppose."

Makes sense. Alex is getting to an age where most kids in the public eye begin to get interesting. Usually because they start doing stupid things. I'm guessing losing a kid sister could qualify him for idiot status in the newspapers.

"How are we going to get away from him?" I ask.

Alex heaves a ginormous sigh. "I don't know. I need to think. For now, let's do what we came here for. I doubt any newspaper will find a photograph of us examining a penny machine all that caption worthy. But we can't be obvious about looking around for Ingrid, all right? I don't want him to catch on that we're doing anything besides being tourists."

"Aye, aye, captain."

I thought maybe I'd get a smile out of him, but his jaw is clenched and his eyebrows are bunched over his eyes. I wobble alongside him into the lobby of Ripley's Believe It or Not!, being very careful not to glance behind me.

So, Ripley's is . . . in a word: weird.

At Your Service

First of all, we're greeted by two life-sized mannequins that look like the fake people on the Pirates of the Caribbean ride at the Magic Kingdom. Except instead of being dressed up as pirates, one is wearing a cowboy getup and the other is . . . well . . . the other is a bearded lady. To be more specific, she is Sexy Sadie the Bearded Lady. Or so the sign above her says.

So yeah . . . weird.

Behind those two is the gift shop, and to the side of the gift shop entrance is the penny machine. It's there, but Ingrid is not. Right on trend with the day. All the hope I've been holding on to seeps out of me like a balloon losing air. It's official, we are never finding her. But I can't say that to Alex. Well, obviously, I wouldn't say it anyway, because it's his sister we're talking about and I need to stay positive in front of him. But I also can't say it because we're being trailed by a paparazzo, and if that guy broke the story on CNN or something that would be . . . not good.

Clearly Alex is seeing what I'm seeing, or rather, what I'm not seeing. His shoulders sag and then his head gives a little nod, like he's giving himself a pep talk in his mind.

He turns to face me. "Will you be all right on your own for a second? Can you stand without my help?"

"Sure, but why? Where are you going?"

Alex looks like he's ready to concede defeat. He also looks really, really tired.

"I'm planning to converse with the leech." He gestures with his head to the guy with a camera behind him. Now that I'm facing Alex, I get my first good look at the photographer. He looks sleazy, like the kind of dude you'd expect to be skulking in the shadows, just waiting to jump out with his camera. He has on an olive-green vest with about a zillion pockets, the kind people wear on safari or to go fishing, and his hair is slicked back with something oily. Or maybe he just hasn't washed it in a long time. His head is ducked down, but I can tell that he's watching us out of the corners of his eyes. Yuck.

"Um, okay. What are you going to say?" I ask.

Alex gives me a watered-down version of his lopsided grin and shrugs. It doesn't make me feel better.

"I'll handle it. Don't worry."

He keeps his hand on my elbow to steady me until I am balancing upright. Then he squeezes my arm and walks purposefully to where the photographer is cleaning his camera lens with the corner of his shirttail.

I should be more subtle, but I'm basically staring and I

don't even care. A few people wander in between where Alex and the photographer are talking and my spot, so I have to hobble back and forth a little to keep an eye on them. Stupid tourists. It's a not-even-real woman with a beard. Haven't you ever seen one of those before?

There is some gesturing going on, but I can't tell at all what is being said or agreed upon. Alex runs his hand through his hair and then he holds out his other hand to the photographer, who pauses for a second, then shakes it. The paparazzo flashes Alex a smug grin like he just solved a Rubik's Cube, but Alex doesn't return it. He just turns around and walks back to me.

As soon as he's in earshot, I pounce on him. "What was that all about? What did you say? What was that handshake?"

Alex holds up both hands. "Steady there. I'll fill you in, not to worry. Though, you'll have to give me your solemn word you'll not be angry."

Angry? Why would I be angry? What could he tell a photographer that would possibly make *me* angry? It's not like I'm gossip worthy.

"Spill," I say.

"Well, the thing of it is, he did recognize me and has every intention of following us around until he gets something he can sell to the tabloids. And obviously, we can't have that. As soon as he realizes that Ingrid is missing, he'll be on the phone to the papers and we'll be in loads of trouble. I don't want Father to find out at all, but having him find out on the national news would be a disaster of epic proportions. I might as well start packing my bags for military school."

"Agreed. So then, how can we ditch him? I don't know how fast you can run with me on your back, but probably not quick enough to lose that guy."

"No, I know. It's not your fault you have a twisted ankle, but it does make things a little more challenging. We probably won't be able to shake him. But don't worry. I've touched upon a solution. He simply wants a picture to sell. I can give him that. And he's promised to leave us alone afterward."

"Oh. O-kaaay." Still not sure what any of this has to do with me or why I'd be mad.

"Well, so the matter is, he needs something brilliant that he knows he can get paid for."

"Right. So, what, do you need to pose in front of Sexy Sadie or something?"

"Well, no. Not exactly. See . . . ah . . . the truth is, I said I'd let him take a picture of me . . ." Alex takes a really deep breath and studies the painted floor—"kissing, er, kissing . . .

you." His eyes slide up a little to check my reaction.

I don't have a reaction. I'm standing statue still. If I was in Madison Square Park, pigeons would be landing on me.

I've never kissed a boy before. Like, ever. Not even when I was a little kid and we used to chase boys around at recess and try to kiss their cheeks.

But I sort of do want to kiss Alex.

At least I think I do. I mean, maybe not exactly under these circumstances, but yeah, I'm pretty sure I do. When he held my hand on the subway and I got all tingly? That was NOTHING compared to the marching band rehearsing in my stomach at the moment.

"Ah, so is it all right?" Poor Alex. He looks like he just asked me to jump off the Chrysler Building without a parachute. I wish I could tell him how totally okay it is . . . better than okay, even, but I can't exactly form any words that sound like actual words. I also can't look him in the eye. I just nod.

A million and five thoughts start popping up in my head like word bubbles in comic strips.

How much are my friends going to *die* when they find out? Does my breath smell like Yankee Stadium hot dogs and energy bar? Do I take off my glasses? Which way am I supposed to tilt my head? What if I go left and he does too and we crack skulls and it's all captured for the whole world to see? What if I don't like it? What if I do? Did I remember to turn off my curling iron this morning?

I don't know why that last one was there. The most important one runs across all the other thoughts like it's on one of those scrolling messages you see on the bottom of the TV newscasts: Does it count as a real kiss if it's only happening to get paparazzi off your trail?

Through the question haze, I nod at Alex again, and he smiles in relief.

And then I stop thinking at all.

Everything from this point on is all feeling. Feeling Alex brush my arm as he slides his hands around my waist. Feeling his warm breath on my face when he says, "Ready?" I nod one more time. He dips me back a little to compensate for my ankle being off the ground and finally, finally, I feel his lips press against mine.

And then I die.

Chapter Twenty-Seven

Okay, so obviously I don't *actually* die. But c'mon. When a girl gets a first kiss like that from a ridiculously cute and funny (plus sweet and, did I mention, cute) prince, you gotta allow for a little melodrama, right? I'm choosing not to acknowledge that my fairy-tale Disney moment is taking place in front of Sexy Sadie the Bearded Lady.

When Alex gently lifts me upright a few seconds later, I'm a little wobbly, and it has nothing to do with the fact that I can't put any weight on my ankle.

"Er, cheers. Thanks," he mumbles.

"Oh, uh, sure thing." I'm surprised I can even form syllables. Over Alex's shoulder, the photographer waves and flashes me a thumbs-up. Is he applauding the kiss or the fact that he got his shot? Whatever. I don't really care what the random paparazzo guy thought of the kiss. I care what Alex thought of the kiss.

"Ah, so, Chloe?" Alex's gaze is still fixated on a spot on the floor.

"Yeah?" Here it comes. The part where he thanks me for helping him out of a sticky situation and reinforces that, of course, the kiss was all business. A means to an end. A sacrifice for the greater—

"I wanted to say, well, that usually being stalked by paparazzi is for the birds, but today, for the first time, I see how it can sometimes have its advantages."

And then his eyes come up to meet mine, and they have a kind of wicked glint in them. He flashes me his signature grin, and suddenly everything is okay and I can exhale. He might not have kissed me under different circumstances, but he might have. Somehow I just sort of know that. And either way, he doesn't regret it now. I smile back at him.

"So, um, that was unexpected, huh?" I ask. It's still a little awkward, and I don't really know what to do with my hands because they had been holding on to him for balance, but now they just feel like they're hanging at the ends of my arms like deadweight. But at least we're smiling and joking, so that helps with the total weirdness of the moment.

"Slight bit, yes." Alex laughs. "Anyway, now that he's gone off to ring his editor, I imagine we should meet Paisley and Sophie. We're almost late." He's still smiling like a crazy person, which makes me feel like the glowing ball that the Good Witch of the North flies around in is bumping against my rib cage, all warm and bright.

"Yeah, okay," I answer, and my cheeks kind of hurt from smiling so hard.

"Piggyback?"

"Oh, um, yeah."

Alex turns around and squats so I can balance myself on his back. I spare one last look toward the gift shop, feeling a little guilty that I haven't thought of Ingrid even once in the last three minutes. And then Alex is carrying me down the city sidewalk again, and all I can think about are my arms wrapped around his shoulders and how much the cool breeze is making my teeth ache. But even though they hurt, I still can't make my mouth stop smiling.

"We have news!"

Paisley is practically jumping out of her shoes when she spots us making our way up Broadway toward Gap. Her face is shining brighter than the marquee over *The Lion King* (which we've both seen seven times, for the record). Just because we can see and hear her doesn't mean we can get to her yet. That takes another few minutes. There are still about forty billion tourists around, and they're all looking up at the buildings and the lights and the flashing ads versus paying any actual attention to where they're going.

Plus, it's like there's an Elmo convention in town. I swear, I can count six within ten feet of me. Really it's just panhandlers who rent incredibly fake-looking costumes and try to get visitors to pay five bucks to take a picture with them. It must work enough, because there are dozens of characters in every direction, but seriously, they look more like Elmo's estranged cousin who had a run-in with a wood chipper.

And Pay has news? Ha! Wait until we're somewhere private where I can tell Paisley *my* news. Then I feel bad right away, because I should be focusing on finding Ingrid and not on replaying the kiss in my head for the fifty-third time.

Luckily, Alex is more levelheaded. I really like that about him. *Focus, Chloe!*

"What news?" asks Alex, trying to catch his breath. I slide off his back and grab his shoulder for balance.

At Your Service

Sophie answers. "The woman at the cash register in M&M's World remembers talking to Ingrid! She sold her one of those souvenir books to put the pennies in, and Ingrid showed her the ones she had so far. Mostly from the Bronx Zoo."

Everyone's eyes fall on me. I bite back any snarky "I told you so" comments, which I have to admit doesn't take that much effort since it feels like all the breath has been knocked out of me. Ingrid is okay. Hallelujah! I'm very composed when I ask, "Did she know where Ingrid was going next?"

Pay's head bobs up and down and her eyes shine. "That's the best part. She did! She said Ingrid asked her how she could get to the Statue of Liberty from here—"

"—and the lady showed her how on a subway map. The most brilliant part of all is it was only about thirty minutes ago!" Sophie talks over Paisley in her excitement.

All of our energy comes rushing back. Granted, I was already on a little post-kiss buzz, but now it feels like everything is right in the world again. Ingrid is safe, or at least she was a half hour ago, which is pretty fantastic. She was here, she was fine, and we know where she's going. And she's not so very far ahead of us. We all take a second to process this news, and then Pay grabs my arm and asks, "Well?"

Jen Malone

"C'mon, let's go!" I say.

Alex crouches down, I clasp my arms on his shoulders and hoist myself onto his back, and then the four of us take off in a run (well, three of us run anyway, and I ride) toward the closest subway station.

Chapter Twenty-Eight

The ride to the South Ferry station only takes about twenty-five minutes, but I'm fairly sure we could record an entire percussion album with all the foot tapping and finger drumming we have going on in our little part of the subway car. Now that we know Ingrid is so close, all of us are crazy impatient to get to our happy ending.

Until Paisley throws a bucket of cold water over our heads.

"How are we getting on the ferry?"

"What?" asks Sophie.

"Well, we usually take the Staten Island Ferry if we just want good views of the Statue of Liberty, and that's free. But Ingrid wants to get off on Liberty Island, because that's where the penny machine is. Which means she'll need to take a

Statue Cruise. Those? Cost big bucks. We have"—she rifles through her wallet—"five dollars and thirty-five cents."

Ugh. This day is seriously one crisis after another. If we find Ingrid and everything turns out well, I swear I am not getting out of pajamas tomorrow. Movies and flannel, that is my Sunday. I wonder if Alex likes popcorn. *Maybe you should worry more about finding his missing sister and less about your love life, Chloe.*

I know, I know. I need to remember what's important here. First and foremost is finding Ingrid, and second is my reputation as a concierge. Falling for a guest is a big no-no, and it's probably not gonna be helped by the photographic evidence that's sure to come out soon.

Yikes. I really didn't even have time to think that one through. What's going to happen when that picture is all over the place? Oh. My. Gosh. My dad might see me kissing Alex. How did I not think of that? What about my professional reputation? Was I so blinded by a lopsided smile and some dark blue eyes that I just forgot about everything I want out of life? I slide down a little in my seat, and my nervous energy saps out of me.

Tomorrow might not be movie day after all. Usually TV privileges are the first thing I lose when I get punished. As reassuring as the thought of finding Ingrid is, it also makes the aftermath feel that much closer, and I'm finally able to give some thought to what will happen after all this is over. I don't think I even want to know what I'll lose for everything I've done today. I try to imagine the worst, most torturous punishment ever and decide it's a toss-up between a month as Marie LaFou's personal assistant or a year on that island where they imprisoned Napoleon.

Let's recap: offended royals (though at least Alex is on my side now. Sophie might have conceded the point on New York City being impressive, and, granted, she *did* apologize, but she still hasn't really spoken directly to me since then. Maybe the two of them will cancel each other out on their guest comment cards), lost a child (resolution: unknown), and got a picture of myself kissing a hotel guest in the national media (highly incriminating evidence). Maybe Dad and Mr. Buttercup will take pity on my sprained ankle.

"Earth to Chloe!"

I snap my head up at Pay's words to find everyone's eyes on me. Whoops.

"Yeah?"

"Think there's any way we could sneak on?" she asks.

I shake my head. I just took a guest to the Statue of

Liberty last month. They have the same security checkpoints there are at airports. You have to walk through metal detectors and put your bags on conveyor belts to get screened and everything. No chance they wouldn't notice four kids slipping by.

"Nope. Best we can do is hope someone takes pity on us and buys our tickets," I say.

Alex grimaces. "Right, then. In that instance, we should probably plan out which of us should go. Chances are we won't all be able to get tickets. I'll volunteer since Sophie took the Empire State Building."

His logic makes sense, but I hate the thought of any of us being separated after everything we've gone through to get to this point. It's not fair that we can't all see the resolution, assuming Ingrid is there. Then again, it would be really good for Alex to be the one to find her, to show his dad how much of a problem solver he can be.

"I agree," I say. Alex catches my eye and gives me a shy smile. "C'mon, this is our stop."

We exit the subway and locate the entrance into Battery Park. We're so close, I can taste it. I'm riding piggyback again, so I still have my arms wrapped around Alex, and I'm trying to savor the moment. As soon as he disappears onto the ferry, I probably won't get another chance to be this close to him. Once we have Ingrid, there's really no reason not to call Bill with the limo to come get us and return us to the hotel.

Obviously we'll have to come clean about everything, but hopefully, with Ingrid safe and sound, the adults will have an "all's well that ends well" attitude. I can only pray.

Of course, first we need Ingrid. Time to focus again.

"Okay, the terminal is at the back end of the park. Just keep following the path toward the water," I say.

We pass little umbrella-topped stands of people selling cheap souvenirs: Statue of Liberty snow globes and bottle openers and foam Lady Liberty crowns. Hey, maybe Sophie can pop one of those on in case her head misses her real one. There are also street vendors who have tablecloths spread out on the sidewalk where they sell imitation designer purses. We don't pay any of them much attention, though.

Up ahead a ferry sounds its horn as it pulls clear of the dock. Ingrid could be on that boat right this very second. Please, please let her be. I was feeling so good with our solid information, but now a tiny trickle of doubt appears. What if Ingrid changed her mind after leaving M&M's World? What if she got on the wrong train? Or what if someone recognized she was all alone and alerted the authorities? Ingrid could be sitting in a police precinct right now, waiting for the king and queen to come get her. We'd be so dead.

"Do you reckon I can pass for twelve?" Alex asks. I give him a once-over and try not to notice the surfer hair or the twinkly eyes and just focus on how old he looks. Definitely not twelve in my eyes, but grown-ups aren't as good at telling kids' ages. To them, young is young.

"Worth a shot," I say. I'd still rather not risk bad karma by lying, but at this point, with all the "evading" we've been doing, I'm pretty sure our good karma is already out the window. Here's hoping plain-old luck will help us find Ingrid now.

He tucks his shirt into his pants and adjusts his sweater, then tries to arrange his hair so it isn't so messy. "Do I look all right?" he asks.

Pay and Sophie say yes, but I'm too busy trying not to drool to answer.

"Okay, wish me luck."

"Luck." Sophie, Pay, and I all jinx each other.

Alex turns and struts off to the ticket window. I know I was making fun of his "hey, look at me, I'm a prince" walk earlier, but I have to give him credit for totally working it. We follow close behind so we can watch what goes down.

Alex approaches a man about my dad's age. Before he can even open his mouth, the man shoos him away. Strike one.

Alex shrugs at us and flashes that trademark grin of his. He takes more time selecting his next "victim" before he approaches a pretty young mom who is bending over her toddler's stroller.

"Excuse me, madam?" She looks up and her eyes widen. I know, right? Even mothers think he's cute. Or maybe she just likes how Alex looks totally mom approved in his khakis and lightweight cashmere sweater. His manners don't hurt either. And now he's gonna turn that accent on her, so . . .

"I was wondering if you might help me. I was pick-pocketed earlier today, and I'm supposed to meet my parents on Liberty Island. I have a few dollars, but not enough for the ticket. Is there any possibility I could borrow enough for a ticket? It would be my pleasure to mail it back to you."

She tilts her head to the side and studies him. "Your parents left you alone?"

"Yes, madam. I wanted to take some more pictures of the new World Trade Center for my friends back home. I promised my parents I'd be on the very next ferry, and then I realized my wallet had been taken and . . . well. It's just that Mum is going to be so concerned if I don't show up. You know how mothers are."

The woman looks down at her baby stroller and swallows. Nice one, Alex. Way to play the sympathetic-mother card. When I was little, Mom always told me if I ever got lost to find another parent with kids to help. Now I see why. There's no way this woman is not going to help Alex reunite with his poor, frantic mother.

Sure enough, she has her wallet out. "How much do you need?"

Alex smiles and gives her an "aw shucks" look. "Would twenty be too much?"

She hands over a crisp bill.

"Do you have anything with your address? I really will make certain to repay you," he says.

She studies him for another moment, then hands over a business card. Wait until she sees the size of the royal fruit basket she's gonna get later this week.

Alex is sliding the card into his pocket when she says, "Just one other thing."

He raises his eyebrows in question.

At Your Service

"Don't call women 'madam.' It makes us feel old."

Alex smiles and tips a pretend hat. "Yes ma—er, miss."

"Better," she says with a laugh, and goes back to pouring Cheerios onto the tray of the stroller.

Behind her back, he gives us a subtle thumbs-up.

So far, so good.

Chapter Twenty-Nine

We continue to trail Alex to the ticket booth and watch as he talks his way into the kid's rate. He comes back to us with his ticket in one hand and change in the other.

He places $10.20 into my palm. "There was tax, but there's still enough for someone else to come, if you want, Soph."

Sophie looks shyly from Paisley to me. "I think I'll stay with the girls, if you don't mind."

"As you wish. Mine should be the second-to-last ferry, but the line is long, so I think it's going to depend on how fast the security check is moving at this point."

Sophie punches his arm. "Stop talking to us, then! Go get on a ferry and find our sister!"

At Your Service

Alex rubs at his arm. "You didn't have to hit me so hard."

Kind of nice to know royals fight just like siblings everywhere. I've lost track of how many times I've seen Pay and her little sister do the same thing to each other. Alex gives us one last smile, waves, and takes off at a jog for the ferry dock.

"Good luck!" Paisley screams at his back. He lifts his arm in reply and disappears around the corner. For a second none of us move.

So now it's just me, Pay, and Sophie with no Alex to distract me or to act as a buffer. I can feel the tension seep back. Sophie might have had a change of heart about Manhattan, but I'm not sure she's had one about me. I wonder why on earth she wanted to stay with us.

"Should we sit down and wait or something? We can keep an eye on the returning boats to see if she's on one. I doubt it because she only has a short lead, but just in case." I shrug as I finish speaking.

Pay grabs a seat on the closest bench, and Sophie squeezes in next to her. I settle myself in the empty one beside them. It's not particularly hot, but I'm sweating from all the racing around and the anxiety of the day. I might be more tired because of the hopping, but Paisley and Sophie seem plenty wiped too.

We all stare in silence at the woman across the sidewalk. She's dressed as Lady Liberty, but spray-painted entirely in silver and posing as a statue. She's very good. I can't even see her eyes blinking or her arm shaking as she holds the flame high in her right hand. A group of tourists crowd around her for a picture, and at the last second she yells "Boo!" and makes them jump sky-high. When they stop laughing and clutching their sides, they drop money into her hat.

"This is stupid," Sophie says after approximately a minute or so. "I can't just sit and wait."

I was about to say the same thing. Even watching Statue Lady stand still is making me jittery with nervous energy. As tired as I am, I can't stop twitching. "Let's get tickets of our own."

Sophie and Pay swing their heads to me. "Really?" asks Sophie. "What if she's on one of the returning boats?"

"She's not. I feel it in my bones," I state boldly.

Pay rifles through her wallet again. "Let's see, we have—"

"Fifteen dollars and fifty-five cents," answers Sophie automatically. Both Pay and I gape at her.

"What?" She shrugs. "You said on the subway you had five dollars and thirty-five cents, and Alex just handed Chloe ten dollars and twenty cents. It's simple maths, really."

At Your Service

She's right, but still. It would have taken me slightly longer than twelve milliseconds to come up with a dollar amount.

"Okay, so assuming we can pass Pay and me off as twelve, which shouldn't be that hard since we've both only been thirteen for a month, we can get three kid tickets for twenty-seven dollars." I still hate lying, but hopefully karma will understand it's practically an emergency. "So we only need twelve dollars. That sounds doable. Alex just got twenty in two tries."

"Yes, but he's Alex," Sophie mutters.

I have no idea what she means until it's our turn to ask for money. We split up and accost everyone who crosses our path.

"No, sorry, I don't give handouts." Really? Does Sophie look like a street urchin in her designer sundress?

"I just spent my last five. Sorry." Paisley gets nowhere either.

"Excuse me, sir? Sir? Sir, I—well, good day to you too." *Jerk,* I want to add.

It turns out that being really excellent at asking people for favors, like I've done almost weekly since starting as junior concierge, does not translate to mad skills when asking people flat-out for money. It's not like these people care what business the St. Michèle can throw their way. Maybe I'm not as good at this concierge thing as I thought. Maybe it's just that I had a lot to bargain with. The thought is totally depressing.

When we plop back down on our benches to regroup, I plop the hardest. I'm fairly certain I catch Lady Liberty smirking at us, but when I squint at her, her smile is gone, her face is smooth as glass, and her eyes are focused on the horizon.

"We don't have much longer. If we can't catch the last ferry of the day, this could all be in vain anyway." Pay sighs.

I continue studying Lady Liberty, waiting to catch her blinking or twitching or anything. Wow. She's good. Watching her gives me a sudden idea. "Guys, have you ever heard the concept of 'you have to spend money to make money'?" Both girls nod. "I need to spend some of the cash we have. Trust me on this one." To her BFF credit, Pay forks her wallet over, no questions asked.

I hobble up the sidewalk toward the street vendors and hunt until I find one peddling cheap baseball caps. They look like the kind truckers wear, with mesh sides and a puffy front. Ick. But I select a FDNY one and fork over five bucks.

When I return, Sophie and Pay have barely moved. "I hope you brought food," Paisley says.

"No food. Just a hat."

"A hat? Who's supposed to wear that . . . that . . . thing."

At Your Service

Sophie gestures to the trucker hat with her distaste displayed clearly on her face.

"No one's going to wear it. We're going to use it to collect tips."

"Tips?" Sophie asks, but I can tell Pay has caught on.

"We're gonna be street buskers?" she asks.

"Yup." I nod, a small smile creeping across my face. This could actually be kind of fun, if it works.

Then Pay asks the question I've been pushing down ever since I had the idea.

"Um, Chloe, do any of us have any skills worthy of a street performance?"

Chapter Thirty

Okay, so I actually was thinking about possible skills the whole time I shopped for hats, and I have an answer all ready for Paisley.

"Our Broadway medley."

Pay doesn't have quite the reaction I'm hoping for. First she laughs. Then she snorts. Then she sees that I'm serious and her face falls.

"Uh, no. Just . . . no."

"Why, what's wrong with our Broadway medley?" I turn to Sophie to explain. "Two years ago, for the talent show at our school, we did a mash-up of a whole bunch of songs from Broadway shows. We got fourth prize in the singing category."

Pay is looking at me funny as she says, "Tell her how many other acts there were in the singing category."

I sigh. "Three."

"And you got *fourth* place?" I can tell Sophie is trying not to giggle.

"Exactly," says Pay.

"We weren't *that* bad," I mumble. "And I can see you, Pay." She's standing off to the side rotating her finger next to her ear in the universal "she's crazy" sign.

"We were worse," Paisley says.

Sophie is full-out laughing now. I honestly think it might be the first time I've seen this. "Will you show me? Oh, please."

"Of course we will. And you'll see it's not bad at all." I make a big show of placing the hat top down on the ground in front of us, all ready to collect tips. Then I strip off my suit jacket and hand it to Sophie. Pay looks resigned as she assumes her starting position just behind me. Sophie scoots to a bench across from us, so we can face the sidewalk and, hopefully, our soon-to-be-paying audience.

"I won't be able to do all the dance moves with my ankle." My poor ankle. Even wrapped up tight, it's starting to swell against the bandage.

Pay snorts again. "Oh, I think that's just fine. The singing alone will give her enough of an idea."

I turn my neck to glare at her. "I didn't mean *you* shouldn't do them. I'll do all the hand ones; I'll just have to stand in place while I do."

Paisley bites her lower lip and nods, careful not to make eye contact with me. Well, she can just be that way. I seem to remember her being quite the choreographer back when we were plotting our big stage debut. At least she's quiet as she assumes starting position: feet hip-width apart, hands crossed above her head. "And a five, six, seven, eight."

I face Sophie and belt out, *"They say the neon lights are bright on Broadway . . ."*

Pay pops out from behind me, jazz hands fluttering. *"On Broadway."*

A few people walking by poke each other and whisper. Whatever. Like they haven't seen stranger things today; this is New York City. I begin snapping my fingers as I change the tempo and launch into Daddy Warbucks's "N.Y.C." song from *Annie*.

"The shadows at sundown,
The roofs that scrape the sky."

At Your Service

We belt out the rest of the lyrics while a couple more people toss us curious looks. I hope Pay's game for the dance number that's coming up as we head into the next song, from the musical *42nd Street*. I don't want to crane my neck behind me to see, because I'm too afraid to lose my balance. Instead I give a giant smile to a lady walking by with her dog. She yanks on her puppy's leash.

> *"Come and meet those dancing feet*
> *On the avenue I'm taking you to, Forty-Second Street."*

I might be singing about *dancing* on Forty-Second Street, but the minute I say the address, my mind goes right back to *kissing* on Forty-Second Street. I blush and wobble a little on my good leg.

One guy drops a single dollar bill in our hat as he walks by. I forget to sing for a note or two as I salute him. Okay, here comes the finale. Paisley steps up next to me, and I grab on to her shirt for balance. This is going to be tricky with a twisted ankle, but I slide my arm around her back just the same. When we performed this onstage, we had our arms clutched tightly around each other, but now I know it should actually be "fingertips to fabric," thanks to our Rockettes rehearsal.

Pay begins the kickline and I halfheartedly join in, kicking my bandaged ankle a foot or two off the ground. And forget about fingertips to fabric; I have to cling to Paisley to keep from toppling over. We start singing "New York, New York," and I make sure all my ba-ba-ba-da-bops are delivered with extra-snappy jazz hands. We are so owning this.

"It's up to you,
New York, NEEEEEEEEEW YORRRRRRRRRRRRK!"

We belt it out as we come to a rousing finish. And then . . .
Crickets.
Seriously.
No one even acknowledges our existence. After I put my heart and soul into that and everything! I hop on one foot over to Sophie and give a halfhearted bow.

She sticks two fingers in her mouth and lets loose with a whistle Alex can probably hear in his ferry line.

"Brava, ladies! Brava!" At least she seems to have genuinely loved our performance. Too bad she's in no position to tip us.

Pay looks equally impressed with *her*. "Where'd you learn to whistle like that?"

Sophie blushes. "I don't know. It's just this weird thing I can do. I can whistle like any bird, too."

"Really?" Pay looks intrigued. I grab on to the bench for balance as I lean over to retrieve the single dollar bill out of the hat, and then I sit down on my butt next to Sophie.

"Certainly," Sophie says.

"Okay. Do a blue jay," Paisley requests.

Sophie blows a tra-la-la whistle that makes her cheeks hollow out. Pay claps her hands together. "That was great. What else can you do?"

A guy walking by is being totally obvious about eaves-dropping.

"Try a dove," he says. Sure, buddy. Where were you a minute ago when we were performing our hearts out?

Sophie just smiles and rearranges her face. This time her cheeks puff way out as she emits a cooing noise that does sound a lot like a dove. She probably has lots of them in her castle courtyard. They seem like princessy kinds of birds.

"Sparrow," calls Lady Liberty from her platform. Or at least I think it was her. When I glance over, her face is frozen again.

By now a few people have started to gather near us, watching. Hmmm. Zing. A lightbulb flicks on over my head, and I hop back up. Literally. It's all I can do on one functioning leg.

"Ladies and gentlemen, step right up. The Amazing Sophie will dazzle you with her birdcalls. She'll tweet; she'll coo; she'll amaze you!" Okay, so somehow I'm channeling a big-top circus announcer, but whatever, because it's totally working. A few people stop to watch us.

Sophie looks dazed, but she grabs hold of Paisley's hand for courage and jumps up to a standing position on top of the bench. I catch her eye and she grins at me. Grins. At *me*.

I move the FDNY hat in front of our bench and call out, "She's taking requests. What would you like to hear first?"

A little girl in a yellow dress steps forward with a dollar clutched in her fist. She hovers over the hat, looking back at her mom before dropping it in.

I lean down. "What kind of bird would you like to hear?"

She speaks so quietly I can barely hear her. "A parrot?"

"A parrot," I call up to Sophie.

The little girl blushes and rushes back to hide behind her mother's leg. Sophie smiles and nods once, then closes her eyes and lets loose with a string of whistles that sounds exactly like a parrot. I think. I don't really know what a parrot sounds like since I'm pretty sure we don't have those on the Upper West Side, but people are clapping, so it must sound right.

At Your Service

Holy wow.

I really thought Walt Disney made all that stuff up when he drew Snow White bustling around the dwarves' kitchen whistling to the forest animals. But no. Apparently this is some secret princess superpower. What else is true, then? Can she whip up a ball gown from a few scraps of ribbon? Spin straw into gold? Although if that were the case, I guess we wouldn't need to rely on birdcalls to earn our ferry tickets. We could just set her up with a spinning wheel and stage a raid on the stalls of the horses the policemen ride around Central Park.

I get a little lost in my fairy-tale fantasies and don't notice that our hat is filling up with crisp ones. There's even a five-dollar bill in there! Sophie rocks. Meanwhile, she's all lit up like the crystal ball that drops in Times Square on New Year's Eve. She's actually having fun. Little Miss Perfect has dropped her stiff posture and all her decorum, and she's having a blast puffing her cheeks in and out and pointing to audience members with requests.

How weird. But cool. I like this version of Sophie. She catches my eye and winks.

Winks!

In about ten minutes our hat is full, and the three of us

are giggling like we just met the mayor. Even Lady Liberty steps down off her box and transfers three dollars from her hat to ours. "Well done, ladies." Before we can answer her, she's back up and still as a lamppost. For some reason, this makes us giggle even harder.

I count up the bills. "Twenty-three dollars!"

Sophie smiles. "Girls, I think we have a ferry to catch."

Chapter Thirty-One

I force Pay and Sophie to run ahead and grab a spot in the ticket line. It's already 4:20, and I know what the lines to get on the ferry can be like this time of year. It's going to take crazy luck to get on the five o'clock boat and, quite frankly, we haven't had a whole lot of that on our side today. When I catch up to the girls, there are only three groups ahead of us. Sophie looks upset, though.

"What's up? Did they close?" I ask, hobbling in next to them.

"No. But Paisley isn't coming."

I look at Pay and make question marks out of my eyebrows. She just shrugs.

"I was thinking. I know you have your gut feeling and all, but we need to be practical. Ingrid could be headed back here by now. Your boats could all pass right by each other and then we'd be totally out of leads."

She's completely right. It should have been me insisting on this. Yet another concierge fail on my part.

The line moves forward by one.

"I'll stay," I offer. Partly because I think I should be the responsible one since it's kind of my fault we're in this mess and partly because, even though Sophie and I have been acting fine toward each other the last half hour, we haven't actually acknowledged any of the words we exchanged on the subway, and I'm afraid if we're all alone, she'll go back to being the Ice Princess. Or worse. She might yell at me some more.

But Pay is shaking her head. "No, it should be me. Sophie, Ingrid's your sister and chances are good she'll still be on the island. You should be there for that. And Chloe, you're in charge of these guys, so you should probably have at least one of them with you at all times."

The family in front of us steps up to the ticket window.

Hmm. She's right again. As much as I don't want it to just be me and Sophie without Pay as a buffer, I have to admit, her plan makes the most sense. For the thousandth time today, I wish we had our cell phones on us so we could coordinate these things. Right now I could just call up Alex and ask him

At Your Service

if he has Ingrid and, presto bingo, problem solved. Seriously, how did people exist before the digital age?

The family moves away, and I make a quick decision on behalf of all of us. "Pay's right. She should stay. We'll go. C'mon."

Sophie gives a miserable shrug, and the three of us step forward to the window. We don't see anyone inside, but then I realize the person has just bent over. He straightens and catches my eye.

"Two kids' tickets, please," I say.

"Sorry, girls," he says into a small microphone clipped to the cash register, as his right hand tucks a small CLOSED sign into the bottom half of the window. Now I can only see him from the nose up. But he can still see my mouth clearly and it is saying:

A. No.

B. No, no, no, no, no.

C. If I was any less polite, there would be a C, and it would be: Are. You. KIDDING. Me?

This is like walking to school in February and having to go down a half block from the crosswalk to avoid the puddles

237

of slushy, sooty, melting ice puddles and then stepping off the curb only to land in the dog poop someone didn't scoop *and* getting sprayed by a taxi driving too close to the side of the road. It's too much at once. I'm done.

Tears well in my eyes even as I let loose with a hysterical-sounding giggle.

I hope this ticket seller is a New Yorker and therefore prepared for anything, because something is going down. Possibly me. I falter on my ankle and grab on to the ledge of the ticket window for balance. This puts me eye to eye with the surprised ticket seller.

"Please, mister. You have no idea, *no* idea, what kind of a day we're having. We have to get on that ferry."

He looks so sympathetic that for a second I think he's going to open his register back up and print us off some tickets. But then he just says, "Look, kid, I'm sorry. We're sold out."

"You're telling me you can't find space on one of those ferries for two girls? We're small. We'll squeeze. She can sit on my lap."

"It's not that. We're closed."

I sneak a look back at Sophie and Pay, who are watching with defeated looks on their faces. I must look the same, but it hits me how wrong that is. If I really want to make it as a concierge, I need to be better than this. I need to hear no and bounce right back up, already looking for a new angle. Those two might be resigned, but I am Chloe Turner, Junior Concierge, and it's time to start acting like it.

I may not have been able to beg money off passersby, I may not have been able to keep my guests in my possession at all times, I may not have even been able to step foot off a subway car with any degree of grace and coordination, but I'll move to New Jersey before I let a person at a ticket counter keep my guest from doing something she wants to do.

I swipe the tears from my cheeks before turning back to the window. I square my shoulders and stand as tall as I can on my one good leg. Then I take a deep, calming breath like those people doing tai chi in the park before work, and I look the man directly in the eye.

"Sir, I recognize you have orders to follow, and I can appreciate that, but I would like a moment of your time. If I had my wallet on me, I would be able to show you my business card and prove to you that I am the junior concierge at the Hotel St. Michèle. Are you familiar with our hotel, sir?"

The guy looks kind of baffled, but he halfway nods his head.

"Well, in my capacity as junior concierge I often have the opportunity to escort young guests of the hotel on excursions to the Statue of Liberty. In fact, I've been giving some thought to putting together a 'best of' tour we could offer as part of our package deals to bring new guests to the hotel. Now, I would be quite happy to include your cruise line in that package, but in order to do so, I need to know you would be able to accommodate my guests under any and all reasonable circumstances. You understand that, right?"

Another very confused half nod.

"This could be a lucrative deal for both of us. Our guests have discerning tastes, and I see a real opportunity to align our two brands. Of course, in doing so, I'd make sure that you were given substantial credit for helping to bring about this partnership. What is your name?"

He looks a bit dazzled by all my concierge-speak, which is exactly the goal. "Uh, Richard."

"Richard. Very good. So, Richard. What do you say we start off our long and fruitful relationship with a little . . ." I search my brain for the term Alex used earlier with Pay. Got it! ". . . quid pro quo?"

Richard looks impressed I'm speaking Latin. I have to remember to thank Alex. A fancy way to say "you give me something, and I'll give you something" is going to come in handy A LOT during life as a concierge.

At Your Service

Now Richard has an amused smile. "I see. What did you have in mind?" he asks.

"Well, I was thinking you could sell my friend and me two tickets to the ferry, and I could invite you and a guest to be *my* guest for a meal at the hotel. Our dinners for two are usually valued at one hundred fifty dollars, so I think you'll be making out much better in this exchange, wouldn't you agree?"

Richard smiles. "Look, kid, I don't know if you're feeding me a line right now or not. I can't really imagine anyone under thirteen working as a concierge, but you know what? You got *chutzpah* and I like that. I'm gonna sell you those tickets just for ending my day with a chuckle. That'll be nineteen dollars and sixty cents with tax."

My eyes go all wide. I did it. I did it! I remembered who I really am—Capable Chloe, Concierge Extraordinaire—and I at least solved this one problem. Finally, a mini-success.

I grin and stick my hand behind me. Paisley presses twenty one-dollar bills into my palm. Richard looks a little less jolly at having to count out the money, but he lifts the CLOSED sign out of the way to slide two tickets under the glass.

"Have fun, kid."

I know he doesn't think I'm telling the truth, but just wait until he gets his voucher for a comped meal at our Michelin-rated restaurant*. He won't be chuckling then. He'll be too busy chewing.

We step away from the ticket window, and I accept Paisley's high fives and Sophie's shy thank you. I insist that Paisley take the rest of our money to buy a soft pretzel and a soda while she waits, and then Sophie and I turn and make our way to the security checkpoint.

The atmosphere changes as soon as Pay is gone, but I can't tell if it's hostile or just awkward, and Sophie isn't giving me any clues. We don't speak the entire time we're in line. She does help me navigate the metal detector and hop up the small step onto the ferry. We stake out a spot along the back railing, so we can wave good-bye to Pay as we pull away from the dock.

After a few quiet minutes of watching Battery Park get smaller and smaller, I can't take it anymore. Whatever this silence is, I'm determined to make peace. After all, I have my concierge mojo back, she's my guest, and I owe it to the

---

* I bet Richard has never tried duck confit. Or sweetbreads. Dad almost got me to try those once because the name made them sound so delicious. Then Chef spilled the beans that sweetbreads are actually an animal's pancreas. PANCREAS. No. Just no. But maybe Richard will be a fan.

At Your Service

St. Michèle to make sure she has a pleasant visit, other events of today aside. And, um, if I'm being totally honest about it, Sophie might not have been *entirely* wrong with the stuff she said about me. Which kills me to admit.

"So, that birdcall thing was really cool," I say.

Sophie hangs over the railing a little to study the wake. Or to avoid looking at me, more likely. "Thanks."

She's quiet again, and for a few seconds I figure that's all I'm going to get out of her. Until she says, "To be honest, though, I was rather jealous of your and Paisley's thing."

Okay, now she's just being polite. Polite is better than yelling, but c'mon now. Jealous?

"But we were terrible." I know, I know. I wasn't admitting it before, but I can face facts. It's pretty doubtful either Pay or I will end up with our names on a Broadway marquee.

Sophie laughs. "Totally. But you had so much fun doing it together. Well, maybe not today, but I bet you did when you were in the talent show."

We had. We'd laughed nonstop the entire time. Hey, maybe that's why we got fourth place.

Sophie sighs. "I don't have any best friends like that. We travel so much with Mother and Father that I have to be homeschooled by a governess, and most of the time it's just me and Alex and Ingrid together. In the summers I usually stay with my cousins, the countesses, and they're sort of close to my age, but . . . mostly I'm around grown-ups all day."

I definitely feel that. I spend a lot of time in the hotel surrounded by adults. Except I also get to see my friends at school, and a lot of the time I'm doing fun stuff with the guests I'm "concierging," who are sometimes even my age. And, of course, I have Pay.

This is crazy. Am I actually feeling sorry for a real-life princess?

I steal a sideways look at her. "Well, you can hang with Pay and me anytime."

She smiles as she rolls and unrolls her ferry ticket. The wind tugs at her hair, and she doesn't even make any effort to fix it.

"That would be cool. Maybe we could keep in touch or something."

She wants to keep in touch with me? A few hours ago she couldn't stand the sight of me.

"Um, I'm sorry I was kind of a pain earlier." I figure I owe her that. Granted, I had only been trying to be respectful, but I should have picked up on the fact they just wanted to be treated like regular kids.

At Your Service

"It's fine. Paisley explained to me about your job respon-sibilities, and I hadn't really thought about it like that. You didn't know any better."

But I should have. If I want to be a great concierge, I need to learn to read people. I misjudged Sophie, I didn't pay enough attention to Ingrid to know how serious she was about the pennies, and I thought Alex was cocky just because he flips his hair a lot. Basically, without my slam books telling me everything I need to know about a guest, I'm not so hot at figuring out what people want. I guess I need to work on that.

But really, the way I feel now has nothing to do with my wanting to be a great concierge. I want to be nice to Sophie just because I like her and I think she'll be a fun friend. Plus, you never know when you'll need help summoning a carrier pigeon.

"Friends?" I ask, holding out my free hand.

She grins. "Friends." But instead of shaking my hand, she throws her arms around me in a giant, very unprincess-like hug.

Chapter Thirty-Two

Fifteen minutes later we're jockeying for exit position as the ferry ties up on Liberty Island.

You hear stories about how immigrants felt when their boats came into view of the Statue of Liberty and how they got down and kissed the ground when they landed because they knew their dreams could all come true here in America.

I am totally fine with kissing the ground if we find Ingrid here. That's the only American dream I have at the moment. I can tell Sophie is feeling the same way, because she's resumed shredding her ferry ticket and she can't stop bouncing. Seeing as how I'm holding on to her for balance, it's not the most comfortable thing.

At Your Service

"Well, this is it," I say, and she grimaces in reply. She rises up on tiptoes to try to catch a glimpse onto the island, but the boat is low in the water and there's a covered dock that is blocking most everything on land from sight.

We step off the ferry and, I swear, if Sophie were strong enough to carry me, I know she would have tried. I feel like I have a Doberman on a leash, and I'm trying to keep her from racing off without me. What happened to the composed, regal princess from this morning?

"Do you want to run ahead?" I ask.

She looks genuinely ashamed. "No, sorry. I'm just really edgy. I'll slow down."

She offers me her arm again, and I use it to help me hop along. We reach the end and step onto a paved pathway. The statue is all majestic-looking off to our right, but we're both focused on the path to the visitors' center ahead. A guy on the ferry told us the penny machine is in a big, tented gift shop behind the visitors' center, and we make a beeline for it.

I scan left to right the whole way, searching for signs of Alex or Ingrid, but it's just random tourists. *That's okay. They're at the penny machine. Just get to the penny machine.* I have to believe this. After everything we've gone through to get here, it will be too cruel if she isn't there.

The white tent comes into view, and Sophie makes a little sound in her throat. I try to hop faster. We enter the gift shop and look around. Right away I spot the machine in the back corner of the shop and point it out to Sophie. I try not to notice there are no kids, royal or otherwise, crowded around it. But I can't keep a giant lump from forming in my throat. We reach the machine and stop.

Neither of us makes eye contact with the other, because then we'd have to acknowledge the truth.

No Alex. No Ingrid.

I stare at the floor.

"Looking for someone?"

I turn so fast that I forget my ankle, and a surge of pain shoots up my leg.

"Dad?"

Chapter Thirty-Three

Chloe. Got anything you'd like to share about your day?"

Okay, so you know how thirteen-year-olds are way too mature to run crying into their dads' arms? Well . . . not this one. Granted, I don't run, because my ankle is throbbing like the injury is brand-new again, so I more like crumple, but I'm only a little embarrassed to say I use his jacket as an oversize tissue. Sophie stands off to the side, watching quietly.

Dad peels me off his chest and says, "Let me put you girls out of your misery. Princess Ingrid is fine. She and the king are getting a closer peek at the statue right now."

Sophie stiffens beside me. "My . . . my father?"

Dad nods. "We took a helicopter out here about twenty minutes ago. We were just landing when Prince Alex found Princess Ingrid."

Alex found Ingrid. I'm happy about that, at least. Now his dad knows what a responsible leader he can be, when he needs to be. I hope that's how his father is viewing things.

"Er, is he quite angry?" Sophie asks.

Instead of answering, Dad looks behind him at someone. Alex steps out from behind a giant cardboard Statue of Liberty. I'm torn between running (fine, hobbling) to him or hiding my face in Dad's chest again. Just what you want the guy you like to see: you being a crybaby in your parent's arms. Ugh.

Alex's smile is sweet, though. He doesn't make a big deal about my puffy eyes and splotchy cheeks at all. He just holds my eyes for a second and gives me a tiny nod to let me know everything is okay. Then he turns to Sophie.

"He's not exactly pleased. All right, he was quite angry, and I think Hans and Frans will be getting it far worse than us. But he had tabs on Ingrid all day, so she was never in any real danger. And he *does* feel dreadful that we've had such an ordeal, but he felt it was necessary for us to learn an important lesson that will serve us well in our future roles."

At Your Service

Alex runs a hand through his hair and continues. "After I explained to him why we handled things the way we did, he said we showed good leadership skills. He's proud of our quick thinking and 'the fact that we took the reputation of Somerstein into consideration as befits our royal standing.'"

He crooks his pointer fingers to let us know he was quoting his dad. "But . . . he's cutting our trip short since he feels everyone's seen quite enough of New York at this point. We'll leave tomorrow morning instead of Tuesday."

Alex spares a glance at me when he says this and grimaces, so I know he's bummed we can't really spend much more time together. That sucks.

Except, something he said is still buzzing around in my head. *They had tabs on Ingrid all day. Say what?*

Sophie doesn't seem to register that part. She just looks relieved the king isn't mad. I get that. I can't tell if my dad is or isn't, and I'm not sure I'm so eager to find out which it is. I'm still in his arms, so I feel when his cell phone vibrates in his coat pocket. Dad pulls it out and glances down.

"Your Royal Highnesses, Alex, would you mind giving me and Chloe a few minutes? I think if you return to the ferry dock, you'll find Paisley and Frans just arriving."

Paisley is with Frans now? And they got on a ferry? I thought we were on the last ferry. I open and close my mouth, but don't say anything.

"Certainly, Mr. Turner." Sophie looks confused too, but she squeezes my hand and heads for the door. Alex gives me one last lopsided smile and follows her.

Once we're alone(ish)—if you don't count all the strangers shopping for Lady Liberty playing cards and refrigerator magnets—I turn my face up to Dad and give him a sad smile.

He answers with another hug. Whew. That has to be a good thing, right?

"There *will* be punishments for this, Chlo, but that part can come later. Right now, I want to make sure your ankle is okay. What happened?"

I give him the least dramatic version I can manage, but he still looks pretty upset and pronounces that we're calling in the hotel doctor as soon as we get back home. I nod and Dad sighs.

"Okay, now . . . I just want to understand what was going through your head. What I really don't get is why you didn't call me the second you realized Ingrid was missing."

I drop my eyes to the ground and study the blobs of old, flattened chewing gum that dot the cement floor of the gift shop. "I guess I wanted to prove to you I could handle things."

"Oh, baby. I know you did. But it's my job to take care of you, not the other way around. There were more than a few times today I wanted to call the whole thing off and collect you, but I let the king talk me down. Neither of us were aware of the true extent of your injury, though, or you can be assured I would have. Anyway, maybe I threw you into this junior concierge job without taking enough time to really show you the ropes."

I think of the hundreds, or maybe even thousands, of hours I've spent standing next to Dad at his podium, watching him do his thing.

"No, that's not it, Dad. I just wanted to show you I was good enough to handle things on my own. Like your Capable Chloe. Like you."

"But that's the thing, sweets. I *didn't* handle it on my own. How do you think we found Princess Ingrid so fast?"

I definitely want to know the answer to this one. I know in general grown-ups just always seem to be able to swoop in and solve stuff I can't figure out, like it's the easiest thing in the world, but in this case, I need to know exactly how that was accomplished.

I shrug. "I dunno."

"Well, Ernio called me about two minutes after you left

his office. He recognized Prince Alex and Princess Sophie right away and couldn't understand why you introduced them with fake names, even though he played along."

I bite the inside of my lip.

"And while we were talking, he found your cell phones in his drawer. Care to tell me what that was about?"

I let my eyes go anywhere but to Dad's face. "Um, we thought Frans and Hans might be able to track the signal they send out."

Dad barks a half-laugh, half-snort kind of sound. "No more *Law and Order* for you, my little criminal-in-the-making."

He studies me for a second, while *I* study the ground some more and dart tiny glances at him. Then he continues.

"Anyway, he searched the browser on his computer and found what you had printed. When Hans showed up in the lobby and told us about Princess Ingrid and the pennies at FAO Schwarz, we were able to connect the dots pretty quickly. Then it was a matter of making calls. I phoned all the concierges I know and e-mailed the princess's picture to just about every hotel in the city." Dad closes his eyes and shakes his head with the memory. "Within about ten minutes we had people from whatever hotel was situated closest in place at every one of the penny machines. It only took us a few more minutes to locate Ingrid leaving Yankee Stadium."

If only I'd thought to go there first and we'd skipped the Plaza. We could have found her within thirty minutes of losing her. Like Dad had. This entire day could have been avoided.

Although I knew that wasn't the point.

"Then we just had to locate you," Dad was saying, which snapped me out of my thoughts.

"What?"

"The hotel doorman stationed at Yankee Stadium spotted you four just after he'd handed Princess Ingrid over. Of course, I knew you guys were perfectly fine on your own, but the king and queen wanted a bodyguard on your tail just in case, especially with paparazzi hanging around. . . ."

Paparazzi! My hand flies to my mouth as I remember the kiss in front of Ripley's Believe It or Not! *Please don't let Dad have seen the picture, please don't let Dad have seen the picture, please don't let—*

Dad catches my wrist. "Had quite the day, did you? Not everyone can say they kissed an actual, flesh-and-blood prince, huh?"

I know Lady Liberty is a symbol of freedom and means a lot to a lot of people and all that good stuff, but right now

I would be totally fine with a giant sinkhole opening up and taking the entire island underwater, me included.

Dad just chuckles. "With Mom gone, it's just you and me, kiddo, so I guess there's no way I'm avoiding this stuff. Though I would prefer not to see your love life in such vivid color." Dad turns his phone around and shows me the head-line BRIGHT LIGHTS, BIG SMOOCHES underneath a photo of Alex's hands at my waist and his face close to mine. I'm torn between horror and fascination. But mostly embarrassment of the toe-curling variety.

"*Da-aaaaad,*" I groan, and push his phone back at him.

He laughs loudly now. "So, do you like him? Or do you *like* like him?"

"*Da-aaaaad!*"

"Okay, okay, you don't have to talk to the old man about it. But just remember, we're a team, okay?"

I give a tiny nod and resume examining the scuff marks on my patent-leather heels.

"And speaking of teams, if you want to be a great con-cierge, you're going to need to embrace our motto a bit better."

"In Service through Friendship?" *What does that have to do with teamwork?*

"That's right. It doesn't only mean the way we approach our guests. It also means our attitude toward others in the hotel industry. We may get competitive at times about who's the best—"

"You are," I interrupt.

Dad ruffles my hair, like he used to when I was little.

"Thanks, sweetie. But seriously. We're all a team. We each have our strengths, and we can help each other out when we need it."

I'm not quite to a point where I can laugh about any of today, but I do have to hide a tiny smile as I picture the group of concierges I know as a superhero team, like the Avengers. Dad would totally rock Iron Man. He's the coolest one by far. Who would I be? Definitely not one of the superheroes. Not after today.

I think of my own motto: Go big or go home. It's pretty killer, but right now killer doesn't sound nearly as comforting as In Service through Friendship.

So, ask others for help. I think I can manage that. After all, a concierge is only as good as her contacts, and there are plenty of times I have to rely on someone else to help me put my plans for guests in place. I guess I just have to learn to reach out for it when I've messed up and not just when I'm trying to arrange something for a guest.

Then I think of something else killer. And I don't mean killer in a good way.

"Um, Dad, do we have to tell Mr. Whimpers, I mean *Whilpers*, about any of this? He totally has it out for me."

"This one might be tough to keep a secret. You know how gossip works at the Saint Michèle. But I'll do my best to contain it. Though I have to warn you, that picture's probably already making the rounds in the break room. Don't worry— you just let me handle it."

That sounds fine by me. See, I'm already learning to let someone else help with the problem stuff. After the day I've had, I'm pretty ready to let Dad fight my battles. For today, at least. I bet by next weekend, I'll be perfectly ready to take on the Whilps again. I already have a decent plan I've been working on involving the service elevator and the water from inside the lobby's flower arrangement, and I only have one or two kinks to work out.

But for now, I give Dad a hug.

"Is Ingrid *really* perfectly fine?" I know everyone's saying so, but I have to see it with my own eyes.

"Grab on." Dad slings my arm around his back and helps me out of the gift shop and onto the pathway. He guides me to a spot where we have a view to the statue and points. On a set of steps leading to the base of Lady Liberty is little Ingrid, "walking" her Barbie along the stone railing. Her father is a few steps behind. I exhale.

"King Robert was like a big kid at the idea of going up into Lady Liberty's crown. What is it with royals and crowns?" Dad grins at me.

I have another thought. "Do we get to ride back in the helicopter?"

"Yes, Chloe. Although I don't know if there are enough seats for everyone. And don't get any ideas about sharing one with your boyfriend." He bumps my shoulder.

Oh. Holy. Yikes. Is this what it's going to be like with Dad from now on? Someone shoot me.

Even so . . . "You're pretty great, ya know . . . for a dad."

Dad takes a tiny bow. "At your service, my sweet."

Chapter Thirty-Four

Dear Mr. Buttercup,

I would like to personally thank you for the attention you and your staff provided during a particularly . . . interesting . . . time for our family. Please note, we do not hold you or anyone on your staff responsible for the events of that day, and in fact were quite impressed with the attention and care given to the situation by your concierges.

In particular, I would like to commend your younger concierge, Miss Turner, for her grace under pressure, for shepherding my two older children through the city, as well as for taking care of them during what I know was a stressful situation. I do so apologize again for my actions that day causing her to suffer more than was strictly necessary, but I also hope she understands my rationale. Despite a bumpy go of it, she is a credit to your hotel. I hope her injury has thoroughly healed.

If you would be so kind, I'd like to request you pass along some personal messages from my children to Miss Turner:

A. Ingrid wanted me to let Chloe know she found a machine in the London airport that presses euros, and she now has a whole new collection to start. She thought Chloe would be quite excited for her. I'm not sure the rest of us share this enthusiasm, but we shall muddle on.

B. Sophie is hoping Chloe will be pleased to have us stay at the St. Michèle on our next visit to New York, though I can't say for sure when that will be. Chloe made quite an impression on her, and Sophie thinks she's, and I quote, "really cool."

C. Alex requests that you allow us to set up a Skype account for Chloe ASAP, so that they might continue to chat online. We will, of course, make certain it is a secure line, safe from those pesky tabloid reporters.

D. Well, I really don't have a D, but I rather feel lists aren't complete with only an A–C. Wouldn't you quite agree?

Yours in service,

His Royal Highness, King by the Grace of God, Grand Duke of Shenkenburg, Duke of Astoria, Count Palatine of the Rhine, Count of Sasr, Romitostein, Westlundair, and Chern, Burgrave of Galenstein, Lord of Rewerberg, Maculbaden, Bergerstein, Roslinberg, Lumburg, and Appelstein.

a.k.a. your humble servant,

King Robert

Chlo—

I can't stop thinking about Sadie the Bearded Lady! Think you might be game for another visit to her when I return to town? Sophie and I are already nudging Father for a summer visit.

In the meantime: Skype!

XOXO,

Alex